PRAISE FOR
DONNA GRANT
BESTSELLING
ROMANCE NOVELS

"Time travel, ancient legends, and seductive romance are seamlessly interwoven into one captivating package."
—Publishers Weekly on *Midnight's Master*

"Dark, sexy, magical. When I want to indulge in a sizzling fantasy adventure, I read Donna Grant."
—Allison Brennan, New York Times bestseller

5 Stars! Top Pick! "An absolute must read! From beginning to end, it's an incredible ride."
—Night Owl Reviews

"It's good vs. evil Druid in the next installment of Grant's Dark Warrior series. The stakes get higher as discerning one's true loyalties become harder. Grant's compelling characters and continued presence of previous protagonists are key reasons why these books are so gripping. Another exciting and thrilling chapter!"
—RT Book Reviews on *Midnight's Lover*

"Donna Grant has given the paranormal genre a burst of fresh air..."
—San Francisco Book Review

ALSO FROM DONNA GRANT

CONTEMPORARY PARANORMAL

REAPER SERIES
Dark Alpha's Claim
Dark Alpha's Embrace
Dark Alpha's Demand
Dark Alpha's Lover
Tall, Dark, Deadly Alpha Bundle
Dark Alpha's Night (March 2018)
Dark Alpha's Hunger (August 2018)

DARK KING SERIES
Dark Heat (3 novella compilation)
Darkest Flame
Fire Rising
Burning Desire
Hot Blooded
Night's Blaze
Soul Scorched
Dragon King (novella)
Passion Ignites
Smoldering Hunger
Smoke and Fire
Dragon Fever (novella)
Firestorm
Blaze
Dragon Burn (novella)

Constantine: A History (short story)
Heat (January 2018)
Torched (May 2018)

DARK WARRIOR SERIES
Midnight's Master
Midnight's Lover
Midnight's Seduction
Midnight's Warrior
Midnight's Kiss
Midnight's Captive
Midnight's Temptation
Midnight's Promise
Midnight's Surrender (novella)
Dark Warrior Box Set

CHIASSON SERIES
Wild Fever
Wild Dream
Wild Need
Wild Flame
Wild Rapture

LaRUE SERIES
Moon Kissed
Moon Thrall
Moon Struck
Moon Bound

WICKED TREASSURES
Seized by Passion
Enticed by Ecstasy
Captured by Desire
Wicked Treasures Box Set

HISTORICAL PARANORMAL
DARK SWORD SERIES
Everkin (short story)
Eversong
Everwylde (April 2018)

DARK SWORD SERIES
Dangerous Highlander
Forbidden Highlander
Wicked Highlander
Untamed Highlander
Shadow Highlander
Darkest Highlander
Dark Sword Box Set

ROGUES OF SCOTLAND SERIES
The Craving
The Hunger
The Tempted
The Seduced
Rogues of Scotland Box Set

MILITARY ROMANCE / ROMANTIC SUSPENSE

SONS OF TEXAS SERIES
The Hero
The Protector
The Legend
More coming soon!

COWBOY / CONTEMPORARY

HEART OF TEXAS SERIES
The Christmas Cowboy Hero
Cowboy On My Mind (September 2018)
Cold Night, Warm Cowboy (March 2019)

STAND ALONE BOOKS
Mutual Desire
Forever Mine
Savage Moon

ANTHOLOGIES
The Pleasure of His Bed
(including *Ties That Bind*)
The Mammoth Book of Scottish Romance
(including *Forever Mine*)
Scribbling Women and the Real-Life
Romance Heroes Who Love Them
1001 Dark Nights: Bundle Six
(including *Dragon King*)

Moon
BOUND

A LARUE STORY

NEW YORK TIMES BESTSELLING AUTHOR
DONNA GRANT

This is a work of fiction. All of the characters, organizations, and events portrayed in this novel are either products of the author's imagination or are used fictitiously.

MOON BOUND
© **2017 by DL Grant, LLC**
Excerpt from *Heat* copyright © 2017 by Donna Grant
Cover design © 2014 by Leah Suttle

ISBN 10: 1942017456
ISBN 13: 978-1942017455

Available in ebook and print editions

www.DonnaGrant.com
www.MotherofDragonsBooks.com

PRONUNCIATIONS & GLOSSARY

GLOSSARY:

Andouille (*ahn-doo-ee*) & **Boudin** (*boo-dan*)
Two types of Cajun sausage. Andouille is made with pork while boudin with pork and rice.

Bayou (*by-you*)
A sluggish stream bigger than a creek and smaller than a river

Beignet (*bin-yay*)
A fritter or doughnut without a hole, sprinkled with powdered sugar

Cajun (*'ka-jun*)
A person of French-Canadian descent born or living along southern Louisiana.

Etoufee (*ay-two-fay*)
Tangy tomato-based sauce dish usually made with crawfish or shrimp and rice

Gumbo (*gum-bo*)
Thick, savory soup with chicken, seafood, sausage, or wild game

Hoodoo (*hu-du*)
Also known as "conjure" or witchcraft. Thought of as "folk magic" and "superstition". Some say it is the main force against the use of Voodoo.

Jambalaya (*jom-bah-LIE-yah*)
Highly seasoned mixture of sausage, chicken, or seafood and vegetables, simmered with rice until liquid is absorbed

Maman (*muh-mahn*)
Term used for grandmother

Parish
A Louisiana state district; equivalent to the word county

Sha (*a* as in *cat*)
Term of affection meaning darling, dear, or sweetheart.

Voodoo (*vu-du*) – New Orleans
Spiritual folkways originating in the Caribbean. New Orleans Voodoo is separate from other forms (Haitian Vodou and southern Hoodoo). New Orleans Voodoo puts emphasis on Voodoo Queens and Voodoo dolls.

Zydeco (*zy-dey-coh*)
Accordion-based music originating in Louisiana combined with guitar and violin while combing traditional French melodies with Caribbean and blues influences

PRONUNCIATION:

Arcineaux (*are-cen-o*)
Chiasson (*ch-ay-son*)

Davena (*dav-E-na*)
Delia (*d-ee-l-ee-uh*)
Delphine (*d-eh-l-FEEN*)
Dumas (*dOO-mah-s*)
Lafayette (*lah-fai-EHt*)
LaRue (*l-er-OO*)

ACKNOWLEDGEMENTS

A special thanks goes out to my family who lives in the bayous of Louisiana. Those summers I spent there are some of my most precious memories. I also need to send a shout-out to my team. Hats off to my editor, Chelle Olson, and cover design extraordinaire, Leah Suttle. Thank you for helping me get this story out!

Lots of love to my amazing kiddos — Gillian and Connor. Thanks for putting up with my hectic schedule and for talking plot lines. And a special hug for the Grant furbabies — Sheba, Sassy, Diego, and Sisko.

Last but not least, my readers. You have my eternal gratitude for the amazing support you show me and my books. Y'all rock my world. Stay tuned at the end of the story for the first sneak peek of *The Christmas Cowboy Hero*, the first book in my Heart of Texas series out October 31, 2017. A Christmas story on Halloween. How much better can life get?!

xoxo
Donna

A MESSAGE FROM DONNA

Dear Reader —

I wanted to send a special thank you to each and every one of you for going on this journey with me. I began writing the Chiasson series for my father who kept asking me why I continued to set books in Scotland when I could write about the places that were part of my heritage.

The Chiassons were born, and it wasn't long before the LaRues jumped into the picture as well. I've had loads of fun with this fictional family, but some of the most special parts was putting in locations that I know well from my time with my real family in Louisiana. (My father grew up in Lyons Point, where the Chiassons home is.)

It has been a true pleasure to bring these characters to life for my father and you. I've enjoyed learning about each of them and watching them fall in love – and defeating the villains.

Since MOON BOUND wraps up both the series, it is a bittersweet moment. I hope that this story brings you pleasure since I had so much fun writing it as Kane was my favorite LaRue.

Here's to cozy reading spots and swoon-worthy book boyfriends!

Lots of love,
DG

Prologue

FLAMES LICKED AT HIS FUR, SINGEING IT. THE SCENT OF burning flesh filled his nostrils as he circled his foe. Kane snarled, showing the entity inhabiting the human form that he longed to rip his throat out.

George, for his part, didn't appear to acknowledge Kane's threat. Instead, the man watched Delphine. The Voodoo priestess who'd murdered Kane's parents and wreaked havoc on New Orleans was surrounded by flames.

It wasn't how Kane wanted to kill her, but it would be enough for the bitch to finally die. This wasn't the only battle being waged, though. There was another on the streets, with his brothers and cousins facing Delphine's followers. At least Riley made it safely outside with Marshall.

Kane paused, his ears pricking when he heard Riley shout his name. Being in werewolf form had its advantages. He wouldn't have heard her otherwise. The fear in her voice made him glance around for other enemies. Kane released a howl to let his brothers know he was alive.

He spotted the cracking floor of the building even as Delphine rushed George. They all wanted each other dead, but Kane was no fool. He took his chance when he heard the groans of the building as it began to buckle.

The floor beneath his paws sank. Kane leapt into the air toward George, who was being bombarded by Delphine's magic. Kane locked his jaws around George's neck and yanked.

He heard the sound of bone snapping right before the floor collapsed.

Chapter 1

July

THERE WAS NOTHING MORE ENJOYABLE THAN A thunderstorm. Elise leaned a shoulder against the doorway and looked past the screen to the water falling from the eaves of the house.

It wasn't a soft summer rain, but a storm brought on by the intense heat. The floodgates had been opened, and the ground greedily drank its fill. The clouds were churlish, dark against the bleak, gray sky. Lightning flashed all around, and thunder boomed loudly.

Elise looked out over her back yard to the bayou beyond. The rain fell so hard and fast upon the water that it appeared as if the bayou were alive. The roar of the rain was comforting, the storm exhilarating.

A decidedly nice change from her quiet life.

She looked over her shoulder at the Siamese cat curled up

on the back of the sofa, his blue eyes gazing with disdain at the weather. As soon as the cat rushed into the house earlier, Elise had known a storm was headed her way.

While Mr. Darcy liked to spend time outside, he preferred the comfort of being inside at night and anytime there was a storm. The scars on his face and ears proved that he was quite the scrapper—even against the animals of the swamp.

But at least the cat was smart enough to stay far away from the gators.

Elise chuckled and turned her gaze back out to the rain when Mr. Darcy yawned and put a paw over his eyes to sleep. She found her eyes scanning the area for signs of the black dog she'd spotted over the last few weeks. It was huge. At first, she'd thought it a wolf, but there were no wolves in Louisiana.

She'd left a bowl of food out for it, but so far, only the raccoons had enjoyed the meal. The last time she'd seen the dog, he was limping. It had been dusk, so she hadn't been able to see his wound, but it needed to be cleaned before it got infected—and the beautiful dog became a meal for something else.

While she enjoyed the storm, it was messing with her routine. All her life, she'd been a bit OCD with things. And once she made her daily schedule, she hated when things interfered or prevented her from keeping to it.

After three years in the bayou, she should've been used to her perfectly planned days going to shit, but she couldn't quite manage it. At least she no longer fretted about it—as much.

"One day changed both of our lives, Mr. Darcy," she said, though the cat wasn't listening.

Elise had gotten into the habit of talking to the cat, and sometimes, Mr. Darcy would stare at her as if he knew exactly what she said.

It wasn't often that Elise thought of the day that had altered her life so drastically, but when she did, it was hard to shake off the memories. Or the horror of it all.

Her gaze lowered to the scars on her arms that she kept hidden with long sleeves. They were a constant reminder of how close to death she'd come.

But they couldn't compare to the scars inside her.

She ran her hand down her arm, feeling the raised remnants through the linen of her shirt. It was silly to keep them hidden. Many in the small community had seen them already. Because they were the ones who'd saved her.

Elise swallowed as she recalled waking up delirious from a fever, to find herself in a place that would've sent her running if she'd been able.

Thankfully, her injuries, as well as several pairs of hands, kept her on the table. Elise had drifted in and out of consciousness. One time, she'd opened her eyes to see an old Creole woman tending to one of the many cuts on her body.

"Be easy, child," she'd told Elise in a calm, assertive voice.

Elise had looked into the woman's black eyes and saw kindness and wisdom. The next time she woke, Elise found herself staring up at dried herbs, bones strung together and clacking with the wind, as well as the jawbones of several various-sized alligators.

Miss Babette used her skills and knowledge of herbal medicine that had been passed down through generations of her family to tend to Elise's injuries.

It took weeks of convalescing in Babette's house for Elise to heal. She'd learned to shell peas, often woke to the smell of freshly baked bread, and discovered that the slow pace and quiet of the bayou suited her.

Elise never returned to New Orleans after that. She bought a small house and continued her veterinarian practice in the bayou. Instead of the nice sums of money she used to make, she accepted food and other goods in exchange for her services.

And she found contentment.

It wasn't the grand life she'd imagined for herself, but it was a good one. She had true friends who cared about her. Instead of having neighbors she rarely saw and never spoke with in a city, those around her visited often, and there was no going to the store without running into someone and sharing a thirty-minute conversation.

It wasn't just time that moved differently here, the people did, as well. They preferred companionship and waving to each other as you drove down the road to the hustle and bustle of the city, where everyone was chained to their electronics.

Her clientele included cats and dogs but had also expanded

to include cattle, horses, goats, chickens, sheep, and pigs, among other animals. Every day was an adventure, but she was safe. And that's what counted.

Her phone rang, drawing her attention from the storm. She walked to the old rotary phone that hung on the kitchen wall and answered it.

Elise smiled as soon as she heard Ed Perkins' aged voice on the other end of the line. "It's best for you not to venture out for our appointment. I don't like the idea of you driving in this weather."

"It's just a little storm."

"Don't make an old man worry," he replied tersely. "I'll call tomorrow to reschedule."

"Yes, sir."

There was a pause before he asked, "Do you need anything, girl?"

She grinned. "I'm good, thanks."

"Remember, now. Stay indoors. Don't you go out after some animal until the rain stops. It's gonna be a bad one. Heed my words."

"I will, Mr. Perkins."

She hung up the phone and shook her head. Despite giving her cell phone number out, many of the older folks preferred to call the house.

Mr. Perkins had lost his daughter to a head-on collision fifteen years before, and he often called to check on Elise. His fatherly attention was sweet. Especially since her own father was dead.

Elise walked to the fridge and took out the fresh beans Mrs. Baker had given her and began setting out the ingredients for red beans and rice. It was the perfect meal to cook all day in the Crock-Pot for dinner.

When she finished getting everything ready and into the slow cooker, she turned it on and headed to the corner of her small living room where she'd set up a desk.

After checking her planner, she began making calls to her clients to confirm scheduled appointments. Not a single person wanted to keep theirs. For the next thirty minutes, Elise rescheduled everyone.

It was rare for her to have a day to herself during the week. Well, even on the weekend, if she were honest. The lifestyle everyone led here didn't go by the usual times in the city. Few made appointments. Most just called or showed up with whatever animal was in need.

But Elise was going to take advantage of the storm. She set her pencil down, closed her laptop, and pushed back from the desk. She grabbed the top book on the stack that kept growing—weekly—and curled up on the sofa with Mr. Darcy lifting his head to see what she was doing.

As soon as she got comfortable, the cat jumped down from his perch and walked in a circle on her stomach three times before he finally laid down with a loud sigh.

Elise opened the book, but before she could read the first word, her gaze was drawn out the screen door again. The lightning flashed, her eyes following the zigzags as her door outlined it.

Mesmerized, she watched the storm until her eyes grew heavy and she began to drift off to sleep. Elise shifted lower onto the couch so her head was on a pillow.

Mr. Darcy butted her hand with his head. She yawned as she scratched the cat, his loud purring making her smile. This was the life. She didn't need—nor want—anything else.

She was doing what she loved, surrounded by those she cared about and who cared about her. She was no longer trapped in a materialistic society, working long hours while trying to maintain a social life. She no longer went to the gym and worried about her weight or if her stomach was flat enough. She ate what she wanted, when she wanted.

In many ways, she was richer now than she'd ever been in the city.

But it had come at a price.

Chapter 2

The rain washed everything new again. Usually, Kane loved a good downpour, but not this time. It messed with his ability to smell. And he'd gotten so close to his quarry.

He blew out a breath and sat beneath a tree. It'd been over two months since Delphine and George attacked Riley, and Kane was no closer to finding the Voodoo priestess.

Kane spent many of his days in werewolf form. His senses were more acute, and they allowed him to track Delphine. Except every time he got close, she disappeared.

He stood and shook out his fur. The loudness of the rain made him antsy since anyone—or anything—could sneak up on him. Kane kept his head on a swivel.

Damn, but he was tired. The injury he'd gotten from a bobcat the other night wasn't getting any better. Not to mention the drunk idiots with their lights off who'd grazed his back leg with their car before he could get out of the way when he was distracted chasing Delphine's scent.

So many times, he thought of returning to his brothers. No doubt they were at the family bar, Gator Bait. He longed to walk into the establishment and gorge himself on crawfish étouffée and fresh bread while downing as many beers as he could.

His mouth watered just thinking about it. And he'd do it while being surrounded by his brothers and their women.

Family. It meant everything to Kane. It's why he was out in the swamp instead of with his brothers. Especially since he was the major catalyst in this catastrophe.

Kane lay down and rested his head on his front paws. He shut his eyes for a moment. The burden of protecting New Orleans and the surrounding area was a heavy one, but it was one his family, the LaRues, had accepted when one of his ancestors married a Chiasson.

The Chiassons had traveled to Louisiana by way of Nova Scotia and France, all to hunt the supernatural. They'd found a small town that seemed to be like a beacon for the paranormal. The Chiassons made Lyons Point their home and protected the residents from the evil that continually threatened to take them.

Sometimes, the Chiassons lost. Most times, they won.

While the LaRues didn't hunt like their cousins, their job could be considered even more dangerous. Because they'd been cursed to be werewolves. The LaRues kept New Orleans stable. All five factions—witches, weres, djinn, vampires, and Voodoo—had to answer to the LaRues.

At one time, one of the nation's largest wolf packs, the Moonstone clan, had made the city their home and helped the LaRues. That all changed when a Voodoo priestess named Delphine decided she wanted to run the show.

She convinced the Moonstone Pack to betray Kane's parents when they were out one night. Kane had known the instant he heard the explosion that it was the restaurant his parents were dining in.

The death of his parents left him and his three brothers vulnerable, and things went from bad to worse when the Moonstone Pack vanished. That's when he, Solomon, Myles, and Court realized if they were going to survive, they had to get smart...and quick.

They grew up overnight. Kane went from being a kid to an adult in a blink. The factions made him and his brothers prove themselves time and again. Hell, they were still proving themselves.

A few months ago, everything had been coming together. Kane met with Griffin, the Alpha of the Moonstone Pack, and convinced him to call the other weres home to take their rightful places with the LaRues. Except Delphine proved that alliances could still be broken and made sure that Griffin couldn't refuse her.

It'd nearly worked, but Delphine wasn't able to get her hands on Kane's cousin, Riley. So in Kane's eyes, that was a big win.

Kane wondered how Riley and Marshall were doing. No

doubt the two lovebirds were looking to their future. At least he prayed they were. He sincerely hoped they weren't focused on finding him.

His eyes snapped open. Though he hadn't heard anything, his instincts warned that something was near. He didn't rise, though he did concentrate his hearing on picking up more than the sound of the rain hitting the leaves above him.

While he didn't see where Delphine went when the building collapsed, he knew she had gotten out since the only body found in the rubble was George's.

Kane was going to track Delphine down and kill her, as he should've done years ago. No matter how long it took. She'd caused enough heartache and chaos to last twenty lifetimes.

Out of the corner of his eye, he saw a black mass that moved through the trees. It had no shape, moving this way and that as if trying to find itself. The edges of the form were wispy like smoke.

But there was no denying the feeling of evil that surrounded it. Whatever it was, it needed to be destroyed before it hurt someone.

The shape stopped suddenly. Kane remained still. He didn't know if the thing could see or hear, but something had alerted it. Otherwise, why would it halt?

Kane stared at the mass, waiting for it to do something. He even drew in a deep breath, hoping to catch its scent, but the rain prevented it. Finally, it moved on, disappearing into the thick trees.

In all his years of policing the supernatural of New Orleans, he'd never seen such a thing. Was it something new? Something they just didn't know about? Did Delphine have something to do with it?

That seemed the most likely answer. Delphine did anything she could to grow her powers in order to claim the city as her domain.

Kane waited thirty seconds before he quietly rose and followed the being. He grew more concerned the closer it got to the few houses along the bayou.

Suddenly, it took a hard left and drifted out over the water toward a small section of land. Kane went to follow when he spotted dark shapes just beneath the water.

Gators. One step into the bayou, and he might not make it out again.

He walked to another section of land but found more gators. Everywhere he went to cross the water onto the atoll, he found alligators.

As if the dark mass had called them for protection.

Kane snorted to himself. He was giving Delphine—or whatever the thing was—too much credit.

Or was he?

He decided to give up on crossing the water for the moment. Instead, he headed back to the last place he'd picked up Delphine's scent. While he might not know what she was doing in this isolated place, he knew it was only a matter of time before he discovered what Delphine was up to. All he could do was pray that he stopped her before she harmed anyone.

Kane was nearly to his destination when he saw the house. He'd spotted a woman once, but he usually kept clear of residences since he didn't want to get shot at.

But to go around the bayou would take time. If he cut across the back yard, it would be quicker. As before, he studied the house to make sure no one was about before he trotted into the open.

He was almost to the opposite side and the trees that would hide him when he heard a sound behind him. Kane whirled around to find two weres running straight for him. There was no denying that they were after him, he just didn't know why.

So far, his hunt for Delphine had kept him out of Moonstone territory, but even if it didn't, he knew none of the weres would attack without provocation.

Except he was definitely under attack now.

Kane planted his front paws and bared his teeth, issuing a low growl. It slowed the two wolves, but it didn't stop them. After a moment, they renewed their efforts.

He decided to go for the biggest first. Kane waited until they were nearly upon him before he moved. He ducked his head and avoided the teeth aimed at his neck. Then he spun, slamming his hindquarters against the smaller, gray wolf.

Kane then latched on to the larger, red wolf's neck and flipped him onto his side. With his teeth sinking into skin, he eyed the gray were, who picked itself off the ground and paced before him.

Kane growled and bit down harder, causing the red wolf to whimper in pain. Kane didn't want to kill a fellow were, but he wouldn't allow himself to be beaten either.

It was the subtle shift of the gray that warned Kane more wolves were coming up behind him. He ended the werewolf's life with a snap of his teeth.

When he lifted his head, the gray wolf was gone. He turned for the next attack just as three wolves slammed into him.

Despite the fact that Kane was larger than any of them, the weres were determined to take him down. Jaws snapped, growls and snarls sounded, and the scent of blood filled the air.

Through it all, he could've sworn he heard Delphine laughing.

That in itself kept Kane going, in spite of the many injuries. He hurt everywhere, but there would be time enough later to see to all the wounds. Right now, he had to stay alive.

Despite each werewolf he defeated, another took its place like a never-ending battle. His enemies came in fresh, while he struggled to stay on his feet.

The sound of a shotgun, loud and sharp near him, startled him. The other wolves ran off, but he only managed to collapse.

"Get out of here!" he heard a woman shout as she fired off another shot.

He could feel the blood pouring from his many wounds. He tried to get to his feet, but his limbs wouldn't hold him. There was no way he could get a message to his brothers to warn them that, somehow, Delphine had werewolves working for her. With the way the weres had attacked, Solomon, Myles, and Court would be singled out and killed.

Just as they had done to him. Or tried to.

He'd set out on his own to bring down Delphine. Instead, the priestess had won again. If only there were some way to get word to his brothers.

Chapter 3

Vicious growls yanked her from sleep. Elise sat up so fast, she knocked Mr. Darcy off her stomach. A look outside showed a pack of dogs attacking an animal.

She rushed to the door and banged her hands on the doorjamb to break up the fight, but none of the animals heard her over the commotion. Then she spotted black fur and realized the pack was attacking the black dog she'd seen before.

The danger didn't even enter her mind when she grabbed the shotgun from atop her fridge and rushed from the house into the rain. She yelled, but nothing seemed to get the dogs' attention. Then she fired off a shot into the ground, not to hit the animals, but to hopefully scare them off.

It worked. At least, it did at first. Then a few of the dogs returned to the black one.

"Get out of here!" she yelled and aimed the gun towards the pack, firing into the ground again.

She didn't want to kill any of the animals, but she would if they didn't give her a choice. Thankfully, after the second shot, they ran off into the woods.

Elise shook the water from her face but kept her gaze on the woods in case the pack returned. Out of the corner of her eye, she saw the black dog collapse. She'd known he was large, but up close, he was massive. By the look of him, he had some wolf in him.

Yet the longer she looked, the more wolf she saw in his features. But that couldn't be right. Wolves weren't native to the area. After her months spent at a wolf conservatory, she knew the animals, and she was looking at a damn wolf.

After several minutes of quiet, she glanced around for any sign of the others. The animal was unconscious, his breathing shallow, and wounds all over him.

She couldn't leave him out there since she needed to tend to his injuries, but getting a wolf into her house and the room she worked out of would be difficult. Not to mention that if he woke, she might not make it out of the situation alive.

Since she didn't know the extent of his wounds, she didn't want to give him a tranquilizer. Which left her few options.

Elise was about to go in and call someone for help when she happened to glance at the water. The rain had caused her to miss the slight ripples, but she spotted the eyes of a gator as it swam toward them. She glanced at the wolf and saw that his back legs were in the bayou.

"Well, shit," she said and set down her gun to grab hold of

him beneath his shoulders to pull his body out of the water and safely onto land, far enough away that hopefully, the alligator wouldn't follow. She saw the blood pooling from wounds on his back leg that had filled the water with smells the gator couldn't resist.

She took a chance and continued backing up toward her porch, glancing over her shoulder to check on her progress every few seconds—not to mention keeping an eye on the wolf while praying he didn't wake and bite her.

When she finally reached the side door that she had put in to lead into the second bedroom that she'd converted for her work, she gently released the animal and leaned against the house for a second to catch her breath before rushing to get her gun.

She was soaked—with both rain and sweat. The wolf was incredibly heavy. She had no idea how she was going to get him up the steps and into the house without waking him.

After taking a few gulping breaths to calm her racing heart, she knew she had to do something before the wolf woke. Elise opened the side door and leaned her gun against the wall as she looked around for anything she could use to get him inside.

Her shoes slipped on the floor, causing her to bang into the stainless steel table. She winced and pushed the button on the side to lower it to the floor. Then she rushed back outside. It would be so much easier if someone were there to help her carry the animal inside.

She was reaching for the wolf when a howl split the air. Elise stood frozen, chills racing over her skin. A moment later, several more howls joined the first. By the sound of them, the pack had surrounded her house.

Swallowing, she lowered her gaze to the animal at her feet. This wasn't her first time working on wild creatures. She'd gone to Montana to help the local wolf sanctuary with the animals for several summers, also helping the ones roaming the wilderness.

But she was never alone.

After so many years working on farm animals and pets, Elise found her hands shaking. She fisted them and took a deep breath. She could do this, but she had to move quickly because when the animal woke, he would tear through everything.

She bent to grab the animal when the fur began to recede— replaced by skin. Before her eyes, the black wolf changed into a man.

Startled, Elise stepped backward. Her heel caught the edge of the steps, and she began to fall. She waved her arms to right herself, but the next thing she knew, she was on the ground with rain pounding her face.

She hurriedly rolled onto her side and looked at the wolf/ man. Thankfully, he was still unconscious.

A howl, closer than any of the others, caused her to jerk in fear. She jumped up and hooked her arms beneath the man's arms and unceremoniously pulled him inside the house.

When his feet cleared the door, she lowered him and quickly slammed the door shut. Then locked it. Her head whipped around when she heard something on her back porch. She jumped over the man and rushed into the living room before softly closing that door and locking it, as well.

She peered out the window to see one of the wolves jump off her porch and lope into the woods. Elise pressed her forehead against the wall and closed her eyes.

After a second's rest, she returned to her work area. She frowned when she looked at her table meant for treating animals. It wasn't long enough for the man, which meant he'd remain on the floor for the time being. She rubbed her eyes to focus and reached for some rubber gloves before she began to see to his numerous wounds.

First and foremost, she needed to stop the bleeding. With so many injuries, she had to look at each one to figure out which ones were the most severe and then work from there.

She had to turn him on his sides, and even his stomach, to reach everything. Elise didn't look at him as a man. If she did, she might call an ambulance instead.

Wads of gauze were all around her as she stitched one injury after another. She had no idea how long she worked. When she put the tape on the last wound, she sat on her haunches and stretched her back.

But her work wasn't finished. She gave him a shot of antibiotics before cleaning up the mess. Only then did she stand over him and see him not as a patient, but as a man. An incredibly gorgeous male.

She squatted down beside him and fingered a lock of long, golden hair before letting it fall. With him unconscious, she was able to look at her leisure, and she found herself in awe.

He had the kind of face that stopped you in your tracks. A strong jawline, and cheekbones for days. A wide mouth with thin lips.

Her gaze drifted lower. Her lips parted when she took in the broad shoulders and rippling sinew and corded muscles of his chest and abdomen.

Unable to help herself, her eyes followed the light dusting of hair from his navel down to his cock. It had been three years since she'd seen a man naked. She bit her lip as she thought about his manhood thickening with arousal. Embarrassed, she continued her perusal down his thickly muscled legs.

He was rugged, chiseled.

Utterly masculine.

Elise blinked as she realized she couldn't stare at him forever. She needed to get him off the floor and covered before a chill set in.

It was the smell of food that first tugged at his consciousness. Kane pulled in a deep breath, his stomach rumbling at the mouthwatering aroma.

Next, he became aware of the soft cushion at his back

and the weight of the blanket atop him. No sooner did that realization go through his mind than pain exploded through him.

Everything hurt. Hell, even breathing was agony.

Kane kept his inhalations even and remained still to try and get the discomfort of his injuries to subside. His eyes remained shut as he attempted to figure out where he was.

He recalled the attack and how the weres had kept coming for him. Did he make it past the house? He feared not. Now he knew he should've gone around the long way. But he might be dead if he had.

What really concerned him was whether he shifted before or after he'd been brought into the house. He thought back to the attack, trying to remember the wolves that assaulted him. As he pulled up the memories, he recalled the sound of a shotgun. That's what broke up the fight.

Fuck. That meant he'd shifted after he was found.

He was surprised his rescuer hadn't put a bullet in him where he lay. Most who didn't understand the paranormal—or were afraid of it—refused to accept that it was around them.

Kane's thoughts halted when he heard humming. A woman. He'd never remained around any of the houses long, so he didn't know if she lived alone or not. He could possibly open his eyes and find a gun trained on him by another.

The real issue was getting as far from the house as he could. He didn't know why the weres came after him, but he knew they wouldn't let up until he was dead. And he didn't think his current situation would change their minds.

The longer he remained, the more danger he put others in. He needed to sneak out and get far, far away from this place and anywhere there were people. Then he'd determine who wanted him dead and why.

Kane opened his eyes and looked around. A lamp near him was on, but the only other light seemed to be coming from the kitchen. The storm still raged outside as drops pinged against the windows.

Then his eyes clashed with the blue gaze of a cat sitting on the back of the sofa near his head. The Siamese let out a hiss but didn't move.

"Mr. Darcy, be nice," the woman said. "Let our guest sleep."

There was a slight pause, and then the sound of a lid being replaced on a pot before the clink of something being set on a counter.

"Unless he's awake."

The cat made some kind of gurgling noise. Kane didn't take his eyes off the feline. It reminded him of the cat he'd had as a boy. A big male that had dominated the area around his family home. No one messed with that cat without coming away with scars.

Out of the corner of his eye, Kane saw a shape at his feet. His gaze swung to the woman. Her chestnut curls brushed the tops of her shoulders, while an errant tendril fell over her left eye. She brushed it away carelessly.

Green eyes that reminded him of the trees after a rain shower were trained on him. They were the color of a churning ocean during a storm. The shade of a seedling as it pushed through the ground. In her depths, he saw strength, determination, and kindness. As well as a steely resolve.

He took in the soft curve of her jaw and her heart-shaped face. Her plump lips were compressed as she furrowed her brow. Something else that didn't escape his notice was the way she continued to tug on the wrist of her shirt as if she were afraid the sleeve might ride up.

"Are you in pain?" she asked.

"It's manageable. Did you patch me up?"

She nodded. "Some of your wounds were grave."

Yeah. He knew. He could feel them. At least the weres hadn't gotten his neck.

"Thank you for helping me," he said.

She swallowed and moved the same curl again before it resumed its position. "Is this where you explain to me what you are?"

"It's better if I don't. As a matter of fact, it'd be best if I leave immediately."

As soon as he started to sit up, she was beside him, pushing on his shoulder to halt him. Her gaze narrowed. "I didn't spend hours tending to you for you to leave now. Not to mention how long it took me to get you into the house. And on the couch. If you move, you'll bust the stitches. Trust me when I say, it was hell getting some of those injuries to stop bleeding."

He blew out a breath and sank back against the pillow. Once he did, she backed up and gave him a nod. He was weak, and that put him at a disadvantage. But he hated putting her at risk.

"They haven't come near the house since I brought you inside," she told him. She shrugged one shoulder. "I have seen them in the trees, though."

"I shouldn't have ventured so close to your house. I'm sorry."

She smiled. "You've been out for hours. Dinner is nearly done. How does red beans and rice sound?"

"Like Heaven."

"Good," she replied and returned to the kitchen.

Kane pushed up against the pillows to see over the back of the sofa so he could watch her as she moved about. "What were you thinking running out there against all of those wolves?"

"Well, to be fair, I just thought they were large dogs," she said as she tasted the beans before adding in more seasoning. "If I'd known they were wolves, I wouldn't have gone." She looked over her shoulder at him. "I've treated wolves before. Though these are much bigger."

He didn't bother trying to lie to her. What would be the point? She'd seen him shift. "We're werewolves. There's a rather large pack in the area. The Moonstone wolves used to call New Orleans home. They returned recently."

She turned back to the meal. "Apparently, there's some bad blood between y'all."

"The Moonstone Pack is my ally. Regardless, I need to find out who these wolves are following and why they targeted me."

A few minutes later, she returned with a bowl filled with rice and a heaping spoonful of red beans and sausage. "I'm Elise, by the way."

"Kane," he replied.

She grinned, the smile lighting up her eyes. "Nice to meet you."

He was surprised how easily she accepted the news about werewolves. That either meant she had some prior supernatural experience or she had knowledge of things.

She curled up in a chair and closed her eyes for a moment before beginning to eat. Their gazes met, and she jerked her chin to the cat. "Mr. Darcy was feral not that long ago. He was badly injured, but for some reason, he allowed me to mend him. From then on, I suppose you could say he claimed me as his."

"It sounds as if you make a habit of rescuing wounded animals," he said, glancing at the cat that had its eyes closed, though his ears moved toward Elise when she talked.

"That's because I'm a veterinarian."

Kane chuckled. "Then it's fortunate indeed that you found me."

Chapter 4

"I'VE NO DOUBT THAT IF ONE OF MY NEIGHBORS HAD found you, they would've brought you to me. Or shot you after you changed," Elise replied.

"Shifted," he corrected.

"Of course. Shifted."

She couldn't stop staring into his vibrant blue eyes. She'd never seen anything so enthralling before. They snagged her and refused to loosen their hold.

And she was their willing captive.

He took a bite of food and groaned, pleasure covering his features. "This is delicious."

She smiled at the compliment. "There's plenty."

He nodded and shoveled another spoonful into his mouth.

"Do you live out here?" she asked, wondering when he'd eaten last.

Kane gave a shake of his head and swallowed before taking another bite.

"So you just wander the bayou?"

He paused with the spoon halfway to his mouth. He lowered it back to the bowl. "I was searching for someone. I've been tracking them for a while now."

"Surely you have people worried about you?"

Kane's gaze lowered to his meal. "I do."

She nodded and stirred her food to mix the rice, beans, and sausage. "Do they know what you are?"

"My immediate family is all werewolves."

"Oh," she said, unable to keep the shock from her voice. "Then why aren't they with you?"

"I have to do this on my own."

She stopped her questions, and they went back to eating. In just a few minutes, he finished the bowl. Elise fixed him another and brought him some water.

In the time it took her to finish her meal, Kane downed three helpings. It was odd to have someone in the house with her, and she wasn't sure she was entirely comfortable with it. But then she realized that whoever Kane was, he'd been hanging around the bayou for weeks. He could've hurt her at any time and hadn't.

She looked over to find his eyes closed, so she grabbed his bowl and fork and headed to the kitchen. She washed their dishes and cleaned up before standing in front of the window to see if she could catch a glimpse of the other wolves.

"You don't fear me."

She turned her head to the side at the sound of his voice.

"I thought you were asleep."

"Just resting with a full stomach."

His question hung in the air. She turned to face him and shrugged. "I've always been better around animals. They understand me, and I them. It's my calling to help them, and I've risked my life many times to do so."

She swallowed before continuing. "When I realized you were a wolf, it didn't deter me from mending you. Then you shifted. I didn't know what to think. If the other wolves weren't howling, I might have left you out there, but I didn't."

"Thank you for that," he replied softly.

Elise glanced away, rubbing her hand along her sleeve. "I live alone. Always have, just not as isolated as I am now. I've spotted you a few times."

His gaze lowered to her arm where she kept rubbing. Elise halted the action and inwardly kicked herself for the nervous habit.

"Are you from here?" he asked.

"I'm from Alexandria, but I've lived all over the US, going to different places where I could study animals as well as heal them. I came to New Orleans about three years ago to help out a colleague at the zoo."

She heard the wobble in her voice and hated it. It had been years, yet the terror of that night never truly left her.

"Someone hurt you," Kane said.

She briefly met his intense gaze. "Yes. I don't know who it was. For all I know, it was someone who followed me out of the city. Or it could have been random. I never saw them. They drove without headlights and rear-ended me, causing my car to spin and slam against a tree."

"A man?"

Elise's gaze swung to him. "You ask that as if you expected me to say it was something else."

Kane raised a brow. "If you knew what I know, you'd ask the same."

"It was a man. Apparently, I hit my head in the crash and sustained a concussion. I couldn't focus my eyes, so I never got a good look at him as he dragged me from my car and into the woods."

Kane's head tilted at her words. "The crash was just to stop you."

She nodded slowly. "I must have blacked out because when I woke, he was cutting off my clothes with a huge knife. That's when I started fighting him and screaming."

"Good for you."

"One of the townspeople saw my car. When they pulled over to investigate, they heard my screams. They called the police before rushing out to help me."

Kane held her gaze. "You were saved."

She glanced down at her arms. "He didn't rape me, no."

"But he did something else."

Elise moved to the chair and lowered herself onto the edge. She pulled at her fingers as she recalled the pain each time the blade sliced through her skin. "He was furious that

I wouldn't stop screaming. He kept telling me to shut up, that it'd be over soon. But I wouldn't submit. He retaliated by cutting me from my thighs to my chest. He was about to slice my face when the sound of the sirens scared him off."

Kane let out a long breath. "Sometimes, I'm so deep in my world that I forget that humans can be monsters, too. Why did you stay in this place?"

"The locals took me to their healer. If I had been conscious, I might have insisted on a hospital, but there would've been news reports and my face plastered everywhere. The locals swear by Miss Babette, even the police. I remained with her for a few months as she healed my wounds and my spirit. That's when I realized that I liked it here and that I could return the kindness these people freely gave me. I bought this house and now use my skills to help their pets and livestock."

Kane shifted, wincing slightly. "And your attacker?"

"They caught him six weeks later after he forced an off-duty cop off the road. She was ready for him, and had him at gunpoint when he opened her door. He's serving jail time now."

Kane's lips softened and curved into a half smile. "I'm glad you seem to have found your place."

"It took a while, but yes, I have."

"With what happened to you, some would become fearful of everyone."

She sat back and snorted. "Oh, I was for a while. I slept with the shotgun and never opened the doors once it was dark outside. But I refused to let my attacker keep that kind of hold over me. So I forged a new path."

"And your family?"

"My father died when I was five, and my mother when I was seventeen. I have a brother. He's in the military and stationed all over the world, which makes it difficult to keep in touch with him. I can't keep track of him. I hear from him about once a year."

Kane leaned his head back and looked at the ceiling. "I've three bothers. Two older and one younger. We have a family business, so we're close."

"Yet you came out here on your own."

"To clean up a mess I helped create," he retorted.

Elise tucked her legs against her. "Wouldn't it get finished quicker if you had your brothers?"

"Definitely. But they have others they're responsible for."

"You don't?"

"No."

She put her elbow on the arm of the chair and propped her chin on her hand. "No doubt they believe the worst. You should at least call them."

"I'll return to them when I'm finished," he stated in a hard voice.

"You sound like Danny. My brother likes to do things on his own, as well. But have you considered that you might not finish for years? Or, what if you die? You nearly did today."

His lips flattened as he sighed. "My family has known

much heartache and suffered greatly. We're cursed to be werewolves. My brothers have found happiness and some semblance of stability with the women they love. I can't pull them away from that."

"Is it really your choice to make?"

He shrugged, shaking his head. "Maybe not, but I made it. I'm the only one not attached. I'm the one who created half of this shit we're in. I've sat around for too long, hoping we'd come out the victors. Many of our friends have died. I almost lost my cousin because of it. Riley isn't just my only female cousin and someone who needs to be protected, she's my closest friend. And she was nearly killed."

"You've been out here for how long?"

"Two months," he replied.

Elise's brows rose. "Have you come close to locating your target?"

"A few times, but she's an elusive bitch."

She pushed up from the chair and walked into the kitchen to cut a piece of cherry pie she'd made the day before. She carried it to the living room and handed him the largest slice along with a fork.

"Then it appears you're going to need your strength."

He grinned and took the plate before sinking his fork into the dessert. She laughed when he let out a loud moan of appreciation.

Chapter 5

THE HOWLS WOKE KANE. EVERY NIGHT FOR THE LAST three, a wolf howled, perhaps to remind him that they were waiting. As if he'd forget.

He'd remained on the couch, only rising to relieve himself and for Elise to change his bandages. But he could feel his strength returning. It was slow, though. Too damn slow.

How much longer would the wolves wait to attack? He hadn't been prepared when they charged him, and now, with him being so weak, he knew he didn't stand a chance against them alone. But with his brothers....

No. Kane couldn't bring them into this. Especially if it was a trap set by Delphine—and it was definitely something that bitch would do.

He looked down to find Mr. Darcy curled on the only part of his chest that wasn't wounded. The cat was never far from him, and Kane had to admit that he quite liked the little rascal.

Kane softly petted the Siamese, waking him. Mr. Darcy blinked his blue eyes at him before rising and moving to the back of the couch. Kane then gritted his teeth and slowly sat up before getting to his feet. With the blanket wrapped around his waist and held with one hand, he made his way to the window. He braced his other palm against the windowsill and stared out into the night.

Shadows cloaked the ground, but the werewolves were out there. The silence of the other night creatures was proof of that.

He might be making a mistake believing that Delphine was the one who'd sent the wolves after him. There might be a new enemy in town. Then again, everything he knew about the priestess pointed to her.

She hated the LaRues. She had gone to great pains to remove his parents, as well as the Alphas of the Moonstone Pack. Against all odds, he and his brothers had survived. Only to continue to battle Delphine time and again.

When would the nightmare end? Kane would gladly give his life if it meant his brothers and their women could be free of such a nemesis. There would always be evil in New Orleans, there was no getting around that. But someone like Delphine was ten-times worse than any djinn or vampire.

"You're not thinking of going out there, are you?"

He turned his head to find Elise standing in the doorway of her bedroom with a floral robe wrapped around her. "Not yet. I'm not strong enough."

"But when you are, you intend to fight them yourself?" she asked as she walked to stand beside him.

He shrugged. "It's me they want."

"It might be prudent to let your brothers help."

"That's exactly what she wants me to do."

Elise tucked a curl behind her ear. "Who is this woman you're after?"

"Her name is Delphine, a powerful Voodoo priestess."

"I take that to mean the two of you have clashed before."

Kane briefly closed his eyes. "Many times."

"And you plan to end it all?"

"I do."

"How?" Elise asked.

He drew in a sharp breath and contemplated her words. "By any means necessary. She kills without hesitation or thought in order to gain more power. My family and I stand in her way, and she intends to get rid of us."

"Because you police the city?"

Kane glanced at her to see a small frown on her brow. "And because we've continually thwarted her attempts to gain more power. We've been lucky. I'm not sure how we won, and I can't help but feel that our time is running out."

"It sounds as though you and your brothers are stronger together."

He grinned as he realized what she was trying to do. "We are, but I can't pull them into this."

"And I won't stand by and watch you get killed."

Kane dropped his arm and faced her, all too aware that he stood naked except for a blanket. The times she'd tended to his injuries, her touch had been light, soothing—and damned alluring. She had no idea how sexy she was.

Or how he fought not to place his lips upon hers.

Elise stood in the soft glow of the moonlight, looking ethereal and too beautiful for words. In their days together, he'd come to see the type of woman she was.

Compassionate, giving, and tenderhearted. She'd stayed up for hours helping a sheep give birth, worked tirelessly to save a puppy who'd shattered a hip after being hit by a car, and greeted everyone who came to her with a warm smile.

While he'd kept out of sight of her clients, he'd heard them through the closed door. They absolutely adored Elise. And he was coming to, as well.

In the evenings, he listened as she spoke of the people and animals she visited and told him stories about the residents while she cooked. After the meal, they played chess or read. Though she had a television, Elise rarely turned it on. And with the hundreds of books on the bookshelf lining the far wall, he understood why.

Not once had she demanded to know his full name or poked into his past—even after she'd told him her story. She asked nothing of him.

But maybe it was time she understood just what she had unintentionally gotten herself into.

"Delphine came to power after murdering the priestess

she was studying under," Kane began. "I remember hearing my parents discuss her at night in their bedroom when they thought we were asleep. They were worried. Very worried. I began paying attention after that and listening for Delphine's name.

"She garnered status within the Voodoo community seemingly overnight. And with that, her powers grew. Other factions began to come to my parents, wanting them to do something about Delphine. But everyone waited too long."

Elise frowned. "Meaning?"

"My guess is that Delphine either learned that my parents were plotting to take her down, or she realized that removing Mom and Dad would make the others bow down to her." Kane lifted one shoulder in a shrug, immediately regretting it as it pulled several sets of stitches. "She blew up the restaurant my parents were eating at, but that didn't kill them. One of her followers put a knife in their hearts."

Elise's hand reached out and touched his that held the blanket. "You said they died, but you didn't say how."

"It doesn't really matter. Delphine was the cause of it. She stood there and watched them die. Then she caused the Alpha of the Moonstone Pack and his wife to go insane, making it necessary for the other weres in the pack to kill their Alphas. The pack disbanded and ran in fear after that. My brothers and I were young, and though we knew our role, we hadn't really gotten involved yet. Solomon, my eldest brother, sat us down and told us everything. Court was so young, he doesn't remember much of it, and we sheltered him as best we could. But I remember every horrible minute of it."

Her hand squeezed his before falling away.

He missed her touch more than he expected. How could someone he knew so little about affect him so deeply? "Solomon and Myles went out to the leaders of the other factions while I stayed with Court. I believe it was that action that saved us. We intended to continue protecting the city. The others feared Delphine, but they didn't want her leading them."

"They joined you, then?" Elise asked.

"Not really. They alerted us to anything they discovered about Delphine, which helped us stay alive. We learned our place quickly and put measures in place to prevent Delphine—or any of the others—from entering our home. That safety allowed us to grow into who we are now."

"Werewolves."

He laughed softly. "With some pretty cool fighting skills."

She grinned at his words. "Obviously, all of you reached adulthood."

"That we did. We couldn't have done it alone. But that doesn't mean Delphine hasn't inflicted her share of horrors."

Elise took his hand and turned him to the sofa. "You shouldn't push yourself too hard."

"I have to. I can't stay here forever."

Her green eyes jerked to his. "I know, but if you want to get healthy, you need to let your body heal."

He allowed her to lead him to the couch since she was touching him again. Even when she was poking at his injuries, he found her soft hands soothing. Just her touch was enough to ease him.

Once on the couch, he lay back as she sat in the chair. She licked her lips and clasped her hands together. "Why do you think Delphine is here? I thought her place was in New Orleans."

"It was, and is. She has numerous followers there, along with a large section of the city. Delphine wasn't just after my family, she also targeted my cousins. For reasons we don't know yet, Delphine went after Riley, who was staying with me. In a battle several months ago where we teamed up with the witches and the Moonstone Pack, Delphine took Riley."

Elise's eyes bulged at the news. "Took her? Please tell me Riley didn't die."

"Delphine wiped her memories and made Riley believe Delphine was her friend. A friend of the Chiassons, who was once a detective in the city, helped locate Riley and get her memories back. But the fallout was another battle."

"The building that collapsed," Elise said as she sat back. "That was you?"

"It was, yes. Riley and Marshall got out in time. I knew Delphine would try something, so I followed her into the building. I intended to kill her, but things didn't quite go as planned. The building began to crumble. I got out, but I know she did, as well."

Elise tilted her head to the side as she pursed her lips. "Are you telling me you've been hunting her ever since and you've not told your family you're alive?"

He glanced at the floor. "Like I told you, it's better that I go after her alone."

"Obviously not, if she was the cause of your attack."

Kane frowned at her words. "Delphine isn't someone who works with others. She uses them. I can't imagine how she got the werewolves to work for her."

A terrible feeling churned his gut.

"What?" Elise asked as she scooted to the edge of the chair. "What are you thinking?"

Kane ran a hand down his chest. "Some months ago, I managed to piss Delphine off. While it was a Voodoo priestess who cursed my family long ago, Delphine decided to punish me by sending me after someone close to my cousins. I couldn't control myself. With Delphine's hex, if I killed, I'd remain in wolf form forever, forgetting who I was."

"But that didn't happen," she said with a grin.

"My cousins stopped me. Barely. And Myles and Court caught Delphine. They had their jaws at her throat and demanded she lift the curse. They should've killed her when they had the chance."

Elise shook her head, her curls swaying. "They wanted to save you."

"And look what that has done. She's targeted our friends, gone after those my brothers care about, and kidnapped

Riley."

"Don't you think all of that has made you stronger? That it allowed you to see Delphine and her motives, her moves?"

Kane sighed loudly, the weariness of the hunt settling into his bones. "I feel as if she leads us on a merry chase while pulling our strings. All we can do is react to whatever she shoves at us."

"And if something happens to you? Will your brothers know? How will they find out that it was Delphine, or learn what you've discovered these last weeks?"

Elise had a point. A good one.

"If I hadn't caused Delphine to curse me, none of this would have happened."

Elise snorted and leaned back, her spine curving as she rested her arms across her stomach. "Seriously? You said that Delphine was after your family. What makes you think any of this would be different? You believe you're the cause, but did you ever think that perhaps she led you right into her trap so she could curse you?"

Damn. Kane had to admit that he hadn't given that line of thinking any consideration.

"That's what I thought," Elise said. She blew out a breath. "Obviously, I know nothing about your world, but I can tell that family is important to you—and your brothers. How would you feel if one of them did what you're doing?"

"I'd rip them a new one," he declared.

She grinned. "That's what I thought."

"It doesn't change my mind."

She pushed up from the chair and came to stand beside him. "You're healing well. I know it won't be long before you leave. I think what you're doing is admirable, but foolish. What you're putting your family through isn't right."

He held her gaze, wishing like hell that he'd met her under different circumstances. He liked her voice, her smile... everything about her. And the longer he was around her, the more the attraction grew.

If he didn't leave soon, he might do something really stupid like take her to bed. That'd be the worst thing he could do since it would send Delphine straight for Elise. And Elise had suffered enough.

Resigned, she said, "You're going to need some clothes. I'll see what I can do tomorrow."

He reached out a hand to stop her as she walked away, but he missed her—and she didn't see him.

Chapter 6

ELISE HAD COME TO ENJOY LIVING ALONE. THE FIRST FEW days Kane was there left her...perplexed, unsure of how to deal with him. But things got easier.

Comfortable.

Elise stared at the ceiling of her bedroom, thinking over their conversation. She'd gotten bits and pieces of his past, but the picture he painted was crystal clear.

Kane and his brothers knew very little peace. They prepared for—and expected—strife because that was their daily life.

On several occasions, she'd found him staring off into space, his mind a million miles away. She wondered what he was thinking about. Or who. The one thing Kane hadn't alluded to was a lover. He'd mentioned his brothers' women several times, but had said he had no one.

But was there someone he longed for? Wished for?

Elise hadn't considered taking a lover, not since her

accident. She wouldn't feel comfortable with anyone seeing her scars. Hell, she didn't like to see them.

But Kane made her think of tangled limbs, sweaty skin, and sighs of pleasure. He made her yearn for something she had forgotten—passion.

Despite her best intentions, Elise didn't sleep the rest of the night. She tossed and turned for hours until she finally rose at five. After a quick shower, she dressed. When she walked into the living room, she found Mr. Darcy once more curled up on Kane's chest as he slept.

She gave the cat a scratch behind the ears, but she didn't touch Kane. Funny how she had seen him naked to mend his wounds, but now she was hesitant to put her hands on him. Mostly because when she did touch his rock-hard body and looked her fill at him, she pictured him naked.

Elise turned on her heel and did some inventory work with her medications until the sun came up. Then she grabbed her purse and keys and walked to the 1990s truck she'd bought.

She drove into town to the thrift shop. Norma, as usual, was already there and gladly let Elise inside. After Elise had checked on Norma's six cats that kept the small shopping center free of rodents, she then searched for some clothes for Kane. She wasn't sure of his size, so she bought a couple of different jeans and shirts. With Norma's help, she found some boots that might fit him.

"Do you have a male companion?" Norma asked hopefully, her gray eyes filled with excitement.

Elise paid for her purchases and looped her fingers in the handles of the bags. "Helping out a friend, is all."

Norma's face fell. She ran her hand over her graying brown hair pulled back in a braid. "Though I never found me someone to marry, I did have relations. It's a good release for the soul."

"Norma," Elise said in mock surprise. "You've been holding back on me."

The woman grinned mischievously. "Oh, the stories I have, my dear."

"I'd love to hear them."

"You need to make stories of your own."

Elise wasn't comfortable talking about her sex life—or lack thereof. She decided to change the subject. "Have you seen anything weird the past couple of months?"

"Weird?" Norma asked with a frown. "How?"

Elise shrugged, searching for the right words. "Anything unusual? What about howls?"

"Like wolves?"

"Yes," she said eagerly. "Have you heard them?"

Norma shook her head and moved the medallion of St. Christopher back and forth on the chain about her neck. "I haven't, but come to think of it, Ted over near you said he's heard what sounded like howls. But that can't be. We don't have wolves here."

"We have coyotes, bobcats, and such. Why not wolves?"

Norma held her gaze for a long silent moment. "I take it

you've heard the wolves?"

"I have." There was no use lying. And besides, Elise hated being deceitful with anyone—especially her friends.

Norma came from behind the counter. "Is your male friend staying with you?"

"For now. He'll be gone soon."

"Hmm. Maybe he'll remain a little longer?"

It was something in the way Norma spoke, but for a second, Elise thought the woman knew much more than she let on. "We'll see. Thanks for these," she said, holding up the bags before walking out.

Elise made one more stop at the local donut shop and picked up an assortment of pastries, as well as some kolaches before heading back.

At the house, she put the truck in park and grabbed the box and bags before getting out of the vehicle. She was halfway to the door when a snarl stopped her in her tracks. Elise looked up to find a wolf between her and the back porch.

Her heart slammed against her chest so hard, she could feel it. Her fingers went numb, and the packages and keys slipped from her grasp.

The wolf bared its teeth and crouched low. Time slowed as Elise glanced about for a place she could get to before the animal pounced, but there was nothing that offered safety other than her truck. And she wouldn't reach it in time.

The fur on the wolf's back stood on end, and right before it launched itself at her, a black blur crossed her field of vision.

As soon as she saw the wolves fighting, she rushed to the porch and into the house, slamming the door behind her. She leaned against it, her limbs shaking at her close encounter.

But the longer she stood there and listened to the fighting, the more she realized that others might join in to attack Kane, and he wasn't ready for that.

Elise ran for her shotgun and opened the door to find herself staring into the yellow eyes of a wolf. She fired the gun at the animal. The wolf howled in protest, blood running from its shoulder before it scurried off.

Elise ran to the edge of the porch and fired her gun again to get the attention of the wolf fighting Kane. The two broke apart, and the attacker turned his gaze to glare at her before it too loped off. For long seconds, neither she nor Kane moved as they waited to see if any others would attack.

Finally, she lowered her gun and found herself looking into Kane's werewolf eyes. They were bright yellow as he watched her.

She shook her head at him. "You're bleeding again."

He turned away from her and picked up the packages with his teeth before bringing them to her. She accepted them, grabbed the box with the pastries, and they returned to the house together.

Kane went straight into her vet area while she put away their breakfast. By the time she made her way to him, he'd shifted into his human form and had covered his lower half with a blanket as he sat on the table.

"I should've looked for them," she said as she stood before him.

He moved a curl out of her eyes and shook his head. "It wouldn't have mattered. I knew they'd try something sooner or later. I've been waiting for them since I heard you drive off."

"Thank you." She lifted the bags of clothes. "I got you a few things. Hopefully, something will fit. I'll take back whatever doesn't work. But first, let's get you cleaned up."

"I busted some stitches."

She walked around him and lifted the blanket to see his left leg. "You busted all of them."

"Great," he stated dryly.

She lifted a vial. "Something for the pain?"

Kane shook his head of golden hair she constantly had the urge to run her fingers through. "No."

Elise set about cleaning him up again. "Whatever healing your body did has been undone."

"I wasn't going to let them hurt you," he replied.

His voice was low, edged with…something. Anger, maybe? The heat of his skin made her hyper-aware of his nakedness—and just how gorgeous his body was. "There were only two of them. If they had wanted to do anything to me, more would've come."

There was a slight pause before he said, "I know."

She stopped in the process of wiping the blood off on his chest to look up at him. "You know?"

His blue eyes met hers. "They wanted to see how badly I was injured."

"Oh." She hadn't even thought of that.

Kane's long fingers wrapped around her arms, and he straightened her. "I've not only shown them that I'm not on death's door, but that I will protect you. That means they'll try and use you to get to me."

"Not if I don't leave."

He smiled sadly. "If only it was that simple. They've been watching the house. They know you're a vet. They'll make sure you have no choice but to leave to see to an animal, and that's when they'll make their move."

"Can't you remind this pack that you're allies?"

"Again, if only it were that easy," he said and dropped his hands. "I've got a bad feeling that these weres aren't part of the pack. I think they're new werewolves, people that Delphine cursed—or rewarded."

Elise gaped as she realized his implication. "She turned some of her followers?"

"It makes sense."

"Dear God."

He snorted softly. "It's a mess, to be sure."

She wanted to urge him to seek out his brothers again, but she knew it'd be futile. He'd made up his mind on the matter, and there was no talking him out of it.

"Have you considered finding the Moonstone Pack?" she asked. She laid a hand on his chiseled abs and cleared away the broken stitches.

He winced slightly when she cleaned out the wound. "I've considered it, but they'll only go to my brothers."

"It's folly to do this on your own. You've no idea how many Delphine has turned."

"It doesn't matter if these are her followers or just people off the street, they're going to do Delphine's bidding. She knows I won't stop until I kill her, so she needs me out of the picture."

Elise glanced up at him. "And anyone you're associated with."

"Which is why I'm leaving tonight."

His words made her freeze. She slowly straightened to look at him. "Please don't."

"The longer I stay, the worse it'll be for you."

"My fate was sealed the moment I helped you, and you know it. You're not ready. Granted, your body has done some incredible healing in the past three days, but you've undone most of that. If you walk out of here tonight, you're effectively committing suicide. I didn't figure you for that."

His lips flattened as he stared at her with narrowed eyes. "Fine. I'll give it another day. But don't go anywhere without me."

"I don't plan on leaving this house."

"Good. Because they could get in while you're gone."

Elise looked out the doorway into the living room where Mr. Darcy was sitting on the back of the couch looking out the window. She just realized that the cat hadn't left the house since the storm—or since she'd brought Kane inside.

"He's not stupid," Kane said of the Siamese.

She turned her gaze back to him. "If they touch my cat, I'll skin them."

He suddenly grinned. "I do believe you would."

Elise became trapped by his hypnotic gaze. She was all too aware that she stood between his legs where the blanket was bunched. She swallowed and looked down at her left hand that rested atop his thigh, so very close to his—

"Something wrong?" he asked.

Elise shook her head and moved around to his back to work on those injuries before he realized just how much she wanted to touch his cock.

She'd thought being away from those mesmerizing blue eyes of his would give her some relief, but she was wrong. Each time she touched him and felt the warmth of his skin and the strength of his muscles, she craved more.

Hungered for it.

Chapter 7

Her touch was agony because he wanted more than just her tending to his wounds. Kane yearned to turn and pull her against him, to cup her face and run his thumb along her lower lip. He craved to see her green eyes flare with unconcealed desire.

All before he put his lips to hers and discovered the taste of her kiss.

His cock hardened uncomfortably. Kane was glad the blanket hid him. Or maybe he should let it fall away and find out what Elise would do if she knew how badly he wanted her.

But the fact that she was again treating his injuries reminded him that things were going from bad to worse. And quickly.

While he hadn't been the one to intentionally put her in harm's way, the fact of the matter was that Elise was being targeted because of him—because she had helped him. He should've left days ago, but he'd let her talk him into staying.

That wasn't entirely true. He'd wanted to remain, so her argument gave him what he needed to linger. He was an idiot. Just because he liked being near her and having her fuss over him, he had all but signed her death warrant.

The fear that had gone through him when he heard the wolf's growls when she returned from town made his blood run like ice through his veins. He hadn't thought twice about exiting through the door she used for the clinic. Or shifting.

He'd gotten there just in time, too, because the wolf had been about to pounce. The sight of a werewolf about to kill Elise made him see red. Kane had wanted to kill the were, to rip its throat out with his teeth and howl his fury to the sky.

The few wards he'd put up around the house while she was gone wouldn't be enough. He would need to add more. Much more.

"Kane."

He blinked and discovered Elise standing before him once more. "Yes?"

"I asked if you needed anything for the pain."

He shook his head. "I can't have anything that will dull my mind."

"At least there are no new injuries."

"It's going to be all right. I promise."

Her green eyes were filled with concern. "I don't want you to go after them. I've...well, I've come to care about you."

He tugged his favorite curl and smiled. "It's because of our friendship that I'm going to make sure they never harm you or anyone else."

"You can't take them on all by yourself. You don't even know how many there are," she argued.

There was a way to remedy that, but it wasn't time yet. Soon. "Did I smell donuts?"

"You're changing the subject."

He brushed his fingers over her puckered brow. "I'm used to my family's worry. I don't like yours."

"Tough. I can't stop it, nor do I want to."

"I'm not the type of person you should be friends with."

She raised a brow and shot him a flat stare. "Is that right? Someone who dedicates his life to protecting innocents? Someone who holds his family close? Someone who willingly puts his life in danger to save others? Sounds exactly like the type of friend I want."

Damn, but he wanted to kiss her. Did she have any idea how utterly irresistible she was?

"Elise," he murmured.

She shook her head, determination in the set of her jaw. "Don't try to change my mind."

He slid from the table and let the blanket drop as he took a step closer to her. She blinked, a moment of confusion evident until she glanced down and saw his arousal. When her green eyes met his again, there was excitement there.

The thought of anything other than kissing her fled his mind. Kane had never known such longing for another before. He cupped her nape, sliding his fingers into her curls as he dropped his gaze to her lips.

They were parted, the pulse at her throat rapid. Desire surged within him and pushed him onward. He lowered his head and was about to kiss her when he heard the sound of an approaching vehicle.

He halted and looked at her. She stared at him with wide, green eyes filled with the same desire that consumed him. With a grin, he brushed his thumb over her lips and gave her a nod.

 She backed up a step before walking to the door when the engine cut off. Elise looked at him over her shoulder before she stepped outside. As soon as she did, Kane grabbed the blanket and bags of clothes and walked to the bathroom.

He was trying on a pair of jeans when he heard voices. Grabbing the first shirt he found, he yanked it over his head. He didn't bother with shoes as he opened the door to better hear what was being said.

"Elise, please tell me," a man said.

"Everything is fine, Mr. Perkins. I promise."

He gave a loud snort. "You fired your gun again, and it wasn't target practice. Norma told me you bought men's clothes today. If there's someone here who is trying to hurt you, I'll get rid of him."

Kane walked from the bathroom to the doorway of the clinic to find a man in his early sixties. He was tall and slim with a full head of salt-and-pepper hair.

"I can promise you, I'm not here to hurt her," Kane said.

The man turned, spearing Kane with gray eyes faded with age. He looked Kane up and down before hooking his thumb in the front pocket of his jeans. "I'd like to hear that from Elise."

"Kane is speaking the truth," she said.

"Kane LaRue," he said, holding out his hand.

There was a pause before the man grasped his hand and shook it. "Ed Perkins."

"A pleasure, Mr. Perkins."

Ed held his gaze for a long minute before releasing his hand. "LaRue, huh?"

Kane inwardly winced. Did the old man know of his family? Surely not. "That's right."

"I knew a Dwight LaRue."

"My father."

"I thought so," Ed said. "I'm sorry about your parents' deaths, son. They were taken too early."

Kane bowed his head in acknowledgement. "Thank you."

"Where are your brothers?"

He narrowed his gaze on the old man. For someone he didn't know, Mr. Perkins seemed to know a lot about his family. "Busy."

"What brings you out here?"

"He's hunting," Elise quickly said.

Ed jerked his chin to the visible wounds on Kane's arms. "Looks like you ran into trouble. Is it the wolves Elise asked

Norma about?"

Out of the corner of his eye, Kane saw Elise jerk her head to Ed. The more Ed talked, the more Kane thought the man might know more than he was letting on.

"There've been strange sightings around," Ed continued. "A black mass that disappears as quickly as it's seen."

That caught Kane's attention. "Where?"

"It's kept to the bayou."

Elise's forehead furrowed deeply. "Black mass?"

Ed swiped a hand over his jaw. "Hunting is sometimes better done in...packs."

Now Kane knew Ed was aware of his heritage. "How well did you know my father?"

"When I was sixteen, I snuck out of the house and took my dad's truck to go meet a girl I was sweet on. I happened upon your father out in the woods being chased by some men. They shot at him, and one of the bullets grazed him."

Kane was taken aback. "The wound on Dad's neck."

Ed grinned. "That's right. I found your father and saw both sides of him."

Elise let out a loud sigh. "You mean you saw him shift."

Ed cut his gaze to her. "So you know. I wasn't sure."

"I'm the one who saved Kane from some werewolves a few days ago," she stated.

Ed blew out a breath. "Being this close to New Orleans, we know some of the goings-on, but not everything. And not all of us. Those of us who do, will help as much as we can."

Kane shook his head. "It'd be better if you didn't."

"When I helped your father, we formed a bond of friendship that lasted until he died. I was at your parents' wedding, and each of the christenings for you and your brothers. I'm aware that your parents were murdered."

"Then you'll understand why I have to do this alone. I'm after Delphine."

Ed took a step back, his face pale. "She's here?"

"I believe she's the black form everyone is seeing," Kane said.

Elise wrapped her arms around her middle. "Is this something she's done before?"

Kane shook his head, thinking back to the last battle. "Remember I told you I was fighting Delphine and George? Neither was concerned about my appearance. They went after each other, sending magic back and forth. George got off one last spell before I killed him and the building collapsed. That could be what turned Delphine into whatever she is now."

"And the weres?" Ed asked.

Kane ran a hand through his hair, shoving the blond strands out of his face. "As I told Elise, I think they're her followers that she's turned."

"So she can still do magic," Elise murmured.

Kane and Ed exchanged looks.

"That's not good news," Ed said. "Maybe it's time to call your brothers."

Elise threw up her hands before letting them slap against

her legs. "That's what I've been telling him."

Kane ignored her and said, "I tracked Delphine. I think I know where she's hiding. I just need to get to her."

"We can help," Ed said.

Kane quickly shook his head. "It won't take her long to realize you're helping. You need to think about your community and the peace that's here. As long as Delphine believes her only worry is me, she might not lash out at the rest of you."

"That's a big chance we're taking," Elise said.

Kane walked into the living room to her desk and grabbed a couple of sheets of printer paper and a pen. He then began to draw some of the basic wards of protection.

He handed the papers to Ed. "Have these carved, painted, or drawn on every building you can. They're for protection and will keep anything evil out."

"And Delphine?" Ed asked.

Kane drew in a breath and compressed his lips. "Stronger wards will need to be added by a witch. Those are basic ones and a few my family learned."

"You should add wards here," Ed said.

Kane glanced at Elise. "I've already begun."

The old man gave a nod and folded the papers before putting them into his pocket. "Norma and I will get this started immediately. Are you sure the two of you should stay here?"

"This is my home," Elise said. "I'm not going anywhere."

"I'll watch over her," Kane promised.

Ed said his good-byes and hurried out the door before driving off. Kane never expected to meet anyone who knew of him in the area. It was a nice surprise, but also gave him worry since Delphine always seemed to find out things like that and used them against her enemies.

"Wow," Elise said. "That's a story Mr. Perkins never shared. And he's told me many."

But Kane didn't want to talk. He turned to Elise and cupped her face with his hands before he leaned down and placed his lips on hers.

Her mouth was soft, supple. He nibbled at her lips, kissing her gently until his need became too great. He wrapped his arms around her and slid his tongue against hers.

She moaned and leaned into him. That's all he needed to deepen the kiss and let the fire burning within him consume them both.

Chapter 8

OH, GOD, SHE'D FORGOTTEN HOW MUCH SHE LOVED kissing. And Kane was a master. His lips moved over hers seductively, expertly.

And when he deepened the kiss...it was utter bliss.

Elise wrapped her arms around his neck and succumbed to the raging desire that surged through her with the force of a hurricane.

He held her firmly, passionately. In his powerful embrace, she felt secure and treasured, coveted even. After her abstinence, her senses were being overloaded with the heady sensations.

She slid her fingers into his golden mane when he effortlessly lifted her before turning them and sitting her on the table. Even through her jeans, she felt the coolness of the stainless steel—a direct contrast to the heat rolling off him.

The strength of him was in every movement. It radiated from him each time his muscles flexed beneath her palms and against her body, reminding her that he was much more than a simple man.

She didn't fully understand the paranormal world he came from, but that didn't matter. Nothing mattered except for how she felt in his arms.

Her head was filled with the sense of him, and the intoxicating passion that swept through her—right up until Kane's hand slipped under her shirt and touched her side... and a scar.

Then reality crashed down on her.

Elise tore her lips from his and turned her head away as she pushed his hand from beneath her shirt.

"What is it?" he asked, his voice husky with desire.

Tears blurred her vision, so she closed her eyes. How could she have forgotten her scars? The very things she couldn't bear to look at—or have anyone else see?

"Elise?"

She swallowed and opened her eyes, but she wouldn't look at him. "Now isn't the time for this."

"That's not what you were thinking a few seconds ago."

His soft, sexy voice was gone, replaced by frustration that edged his words. She shoved him away and stood. "I've work to do."

She walked to the cabinet that lined the back wall and opened it while pretending to look for something. He stared at her for long minutes before he stalked out.

Elise closed her eyes and drew in a shaky breath. Her

scars were a reminder that she had lived through a horrific experience that could have killed her.

But the puckered, raised marks that varied in length and depth from her knees to her chest were mutilations, pure and simple.

While her inner scars might have healed, the ones on her skin never would. The one time she had tried to continue her life as before, it had ended with a child screaming in fear at the sight of her arms.

Ever since, Elise kept herself covered.

She busied herself with patients until lunch. The door to the living room remained shut, as normal. Yet she found herself glancing at it often, wondering what Kane was doing.

After she'd ended their kiss, she hadn't seen or heard from him. Maybe that was for the best. It wasn't as if she wanted to explain why she'd stopped them from going further.

At noon, she hesitated to go into the kitchen to get food because she wasn't ready to face him. Thankfully, a client dropped in with a pet parakeet, and that gave her the excuse she needed to remain.

After that, her appointments kept her booked. She went outside to check on some new baby goats, and when she returned, there was a plate with a sandwich and chips on it on her desk, as well as a *Dr. Pepper*.

Elise knew that Kane was responsible. She looked at the door and hurriedly devoured the sandwich before her next appointment arrived. She ate so fast, her stomach hurt, which caused her to go slower with the salt and vinegar chips.

She had enough time to take a long swig of her soda before the outside door opened and her next client walked in. By the time her last appointment left at 6:30 p.m., she was exhausted.

A quick clean-up of her lab only took fifteen minutes, and then she opened the door and walked into the living room. She glanced around but didn't find Kane.

She smelled something cooking and made her way into the kitchen to check the stove. She found pasta cooking in one pot, and sauce in another. A glance in the oven showed chicken.

When she straightened, she saw something out of the corner of her eye and turned to find Kane standing just inside the back door.

"It smells delicious," she said.

He stared at her a moment before he closed the screen behind him as he entered. "You've had a busy day."

"It was a normal day," she replied with a shrug. "Thanks for the sandwich."

"How many meals do you miss daily?"

She moved out of the way as he walked to the stove and stirred the pasta. "I've got beef jerky I keep near to snack on if I know I'm going to miss lunch."

"Which means often."

The kitchen was small, so she stayed far enough away to give him room, but it felt odd not cooking in her space.

"People come on their lunch breaks if they can't get free any other time. That means I don't get one."

"Maybe you should hire someone to help you."

"I've thought of that."

When he drained the pasta, she got out the plates and utensils and set them on the table. He bade her sit as he dished out the portions for each of them before he joined her.

She took a bite and sighed at the taste. "This is amazing. It's been a long time since anyone cooked for me. Thank you."

"My pleasure. Your house is warded, by the way."

Elise basked in the tasty meal as he explained everything that he'd done to protect her. While Kane was pleasant, the warmth he'd had before was gone. Not that she blamed him. She'd shoved him away without an explanation.

Because she was embarrassed—both of her scars and the fact that she didn't want to show him her body. He looked at her with passion now. The last thing she wanted was to see his disgust or pity once he saw just what that maniac had done to her.

Their dinner conversation was light, as both kept to safe topics. She spoke of her appointments for the coming days, and he talked about the next storm headed their way.

When the meal was finished, she tried to clean up, but he stopped her.

"I've got this," he said. "Go, relax. Take a hot bath."

Which actually sounded good. It took her a moment to relent, but she finally did. She walked to the bathroom and started the water while Kane turned on her stereo that had a Michael Bublé CD playing.

Elise dropped in one of the bath bombs she loved and let it dissolve as she took off her clothes and pinned up her hair. Then she climbed into the tub and lay back in the hot water.

Her eyes immediately closed as she realized just how tired she was. The lack of sleep the night before, coupled with her busy day had sapped her of nearly all her strength. If she hadn't eaten the sandwich Kane had brought her, she would've been dragging by dinner.

With the steam rising up around her, she let her mind wander, and it was no surprise that it focused on Kane. Ever since she'd come upon him in werewolf form, he filled her head.

She'd gawked at his fine body that first day, and then became drawn to him once he woke and they talked. There was something enigmatic about Kane that inexplicably pulled her toward him.

Behind those stunning blue eyes of his was a past he attempted to rectify, and a loneliness that he tried hard to ignore. When he spoke of his cousin, Riley, Elise grasped that he had found someone who understood him without placing any demands on him.

Kane's love for his family was evident in his every word, and every action. He truly thought that what he was doing was for the best.

But it was the way he looked at her that truly touched Elise.

He offered friendship without strings, protection without being asked. He didn't look at her like the victim she was—perhaps because he was a victim himself.

She blinked and realized that the CD was on its second play-through. As she opened her eyes and sat up, she sighed because the water was growing cold. Elise let the water drain before rising and grabbing the nearest towel.

As a habit, she put her back to the mirror and dried off. She didn't look at her body, her gaze instead locked on a spot on the wall as she completed the task.

She then grabbed her robe off the hook on the back of the door and slipped it on. After unpinning her hair, she exited the bathroom and once again found the living room empty.

Was Kane gone? Had he left without saying good-bye? She hurried to one of the living room windows and looked outside, hoping to find him, but she only spotted a squirrel darting to a nearby tree.

Dejected, Elise turned and walked to her bedroom. She stood in the center for a long time before she faced the mirror atop her dresser. When was the last time she'd looked at her scars? Really looked? She couldn't remember.

She untied her robe and let it fall open. She held her own gaze in the mirror, afraid to look down, afraid of what she would see. When she first gazed at her scars, they had been red and ugly.

Taking a deep breath, she let her eyes lower to the scar below her right collarbone. It was about three inches long and angled toward her breast. The wound was no longer red but now faded to nearly match her skin.

That gave her courage to look at the next scar and the next. She was examining her stomach when she sensed someone in the doorway. She looked over to find Kane. By his position, he couldn't see the mirror, only that she stood in her robe with it open.

Their gazes clashed. Her heart did a little flip at the knowledge that he hadn't left yet. Emotion welled within her when she grasped that he was giving her the option to send him away.

Or invite him in.

She looked back in the mirror at herself. Instead of inspecting each wound separately, she looked at herself as a whole. While she still didn't like seeing her body riddled with the scars, they would always be a part of her. Either she could learn to accept them as part of who she was and perhaps open herself up, or she couldn't.

Elise shifted her shoulders to let the robe drop to the floor before she changed her mind. She was terrified that Kane wouldn't like what he saw, but it was the uncertainty that pushed her to take the chance.

A shadow moved behind her a second before Kane appeared in the mirror. They gazed at each other through the mirror. He reached up and tugged on the curl near her cheek that he favored.

Then he put his hands on her shoulders. "Is this the first

time you've looked at yourself since the accident?"

"Yes," she whispered.

"You pushed me away because you didn't want me to see."

She nodded.

His hands shifted forward so that his fingers brushed the scar at her collarbone. Elise jerked and looked away. Slowly, tenderly, Kane turned her head back toward the mirror with his other hand.

It took a few tries, but she was finally able to meet his gaze again. Only then did his hands travel down to the scars on her forearms.

He caressed her body, moving over each wound before turning her to face him. The desire she saw reflected in his eyes made her stomach quiver with need.

This time, she was the one who pulled him close for a kiss.

And she didn't intend to push him away.

Chapter 9

HE'D NEVER HELD ANYTHING SO BEAUTIFUL, SO PRECIOUS. Kane's heart skipped a beat when she kissed him. He wanted to pull her close, grip her tightly, but he feared she would run off again.

He deepened the kiss, letting her decide how close she wanted to be to him. When she wrapped her arms around his neck, her lush body pressing against him, he couldn't hold back his satisfied moan.

The taste of her was sublime, exquisite. He could barely breathe, the need for her was so intense, commanding.

Compelling.

With one kiss, she stole his will, his very essence.

He didn't know what it was about Elise that lured him ever closer. Was it her beauty? Her kindness? Her pure soul? Her smile? Or perhaps it was all of those things and more that he couldn't name.

Her fingers gripped his hair as their kisses grew heated.

Their breaths were ragged, harsh, their need fueling the desire that burned ever brighter, ever hotter.

He cupped the back of her head and kissed across her jaw and down her neck. The moment his lips grazed the first scar near her collarbone, Elise stiffened slightly. To prove to her that he saw her, not the marks on her body, he continued moving his lips over her flushed skin until she relaxed once more.

The woman in his arms was mentally and spiritually stronger than anyone he'd ever met—or, he suspected, ever would meet. She was everything beautiful and perfect, untarnished by the evil that he lived with daily. How could he bring her into such a world when he was stained with blood?

How could he dare to even think he deserved such a woman?

But how could he ignore the pull she had on his heart, his very soul?

He lifted his head to look upon her face. Her lips were parted, her chest heaving. Her eyes fluttered open to show her pupils dilated with a passion so deep, so flagrant that his knees threatened to buckle.

Elise was a dream come true. It boggled his mind that he was with her and that she wanted him. He didn't understand why, but he wasn't going to question such a gift.

He turned them and maneuvered her backward until she came up against a wall. Her green eyes watched him with curiosity and eagerness. He shot her a grin before he ducked his head to continue kissing her body.

Her nails dug into his shoulders when he reached her breasts. Her rosy nipples were hard when his lips passed over them. She sucked in a sharp breath.

With his mouth hovering over a turgid peak, his hand cupped the other breast and massaged it before he closed his lips over her nipple to tease her.

Breathy moans that made his balls tighten filled the room. By the time he moved his mouth to her other breast, she was panting, soft cries of desire falling from her kiss-swollen lips.

Elise was caught in the snug, gorgeous arms of rapture. She burned with need, a yearning so fierce that she knew nothing could tear her away from Kane.

Her eyes opened when his lips left a hot, wet trail down her stomach. He dropped to his knees and glanced up at her, his blue eyes blazing with the promise of pleasure.

She drew in a shaky breath when he hooked an arm behind her knee and lifted it over his shoulder. Her gaze was directed across her room to the window, but she didn't see the curtains or the blinds Mr. Darcy had broken in his attempt to see outside.

Her eyes were open, but her concentration was on Kane and all the wondrous, incredible things he was doing to her.

When his hands gripped her hips, the feeling of his long

fingers wrapping around her as if securing her made her stomach flutter in anticipation.

But it was his warm breath on her sex that made her begin to tremble in expectation. He didn't make her wait long. The first touch of his tongue against her core was electrifying. And hot.

She splayed her hands on the wall in an effort to stay upright as that amazing tongue of his found her clit and relentlessly brought her to the brink of orgasm in seconds.

She remained on the edge until he slid a finger inside her. The force of the climax made her leg buckle. He held her upright and continued to swirl his tongue around her swollen nub until she couldn't stand.

With her body still shuddering from the powerful orgasm, Kane carried her to the bed and gently laid her down. She rose up on her elbows when he pulled off his shirt.

She'd seen him naked several times now, but she'd never get tired of his magnificent body. The life he led was in every honed muscle, every movement. She'd never known anyone like him. Commanding, compelling, and evocative. And for some unknown reason, he was with her.

Elise shifted onto her knees and watched as he unfastened his jeans and shoved them down his legs. A seductive smile curved his lips as his gaze held hers. Then he put a knee on the bed beside her and seized her lips in a kiss that stole her breath—and her heart.

She'd tried hard not to acknowledge her growing feelings

for Kane, but baring her body and soul to him had stripped away all her efforts. And she didn't even care.

Her arms wrapped around him as he laid them on the bed before rolling onto his back. She straddled his hips and sat up. It was then that she realized he was letting her take control. Kane was a dominant personality, but he was handing the reins to her.

Her eyes teared up as emotion choked her. Unaware of her turmoil, he ran his hands up her thighs to her hips. Elise bent and placed her lips on his. If she hadn't already fallen for him, she would have tipped stupidly, crazily in love with him at that moment.

She straightened and rose up on her knees before taking his impressive length in hand. She stroked him up and down, watching his gaze darken as need tightened his face.

"Elise," he ground out in warning.

When was the last time she'd had such control over a man's body? She honestly didn't think she had ever brought her lovers to such a state. Just one more difference in Kane versus all the others who could never measure up.

She brought him to her entrance and slowly lowered herself. The feeling of her body stretching to accommodate him was a sensation she would never forget.

He was burning. The fire scorching him was exquisite, but

it didn't compare to Elise. Her head was thrown back, her curls a beautiful riot around her face.

Her breasts were pushed outward as her back arched, and she began rocking her hips. He skimmed his hands up her back and hooked them on her shoulders as he sat up.

He locked his lips around a nipple and suckled in time with her movements. She let out a groan that he felt all the way to his cock.

He moaned as she scratched her nails down his back. She rocked her hips faster, bringing them ever closer to the pleasure that waited. He both yearned for it and wanted to hold off as long as possible.

Decisions had already been made, and he wasn't ready to think about the next day—or the battle he knew was coming. But he'd already spent enough days with Elise. Delphine wouldn't hesitate to kill Elise to make him suffer, and Kane wasn't going to allow that.

He shoved aside those thoughts and gave himself to Elise. There was a chance they would only have this one night, and he was going to make the most of it.

After watching his brothers each find the women that completed them, Kane had accepted that he wasn't meant to follow that path. Then Elise came along. It made him wish that his path was a different one, but he couldn't change what was in his blood.

He lifted his head and gazed at her face. It was filled with such bliss that it made his heart trip over itself. She altered her movements so she was moving up and down his length.

Every time he slid into her tight, wet sheath, he had to fight back his climax. Then he could wait no longer. He flipped her onto her back and thrust deeply inside her.

Elise let out a loud cry and urged him on with her hands. He began pumping his hips, driving into her hard and fast. She screamed his name as her body stiffened and another orgasm took her.

He kept thrusting, prolonging her pleasure as long as he could.

"I love you."

His gaze jerked to her face at her whispered words, but her eyes were closed. He wasn't sure if he'd actually heard the words, or if they were a figment of his imagination—of the hope and wishful thinking that filled him.

He rose up on his hands and pumped his hips faster until his own climax approached. Stupidly, he hadn't thought about protection, but he wouldn't leave a child behind to be cursed as he was.

Kane pulled out and fell against her as his seed spilled upon Elise's stomach. He'd done many stupid things in his life. But this was one time he had done the right thing.

He didn't know how long he lay in Elise's arms with her hands stroking his hair and back. He rose and cleaned her off before doing the same to himself. Then she pulled him back onto the bed with her.

As if he would've denied her anything. She curled against

him. This simple moment was one of the most special of his life.

In the times he'd taken a woman since Delphine cursed him, Kane hadn't allowed any kind of cuddling. He hadn't wanted that kind of connection with anyone. Yet now, he couldn't imagine not having it with Elise.

He heard her breathing even out as she fell asleep, but he couldn't do the same. His mind was on the following day and everything it would bring.

A part of him wanted to speak to his brothers, but he'd end up telling them what he was doing, and it would defeat his purpose. Instead, he'd leave them a letter. It wouldn't be the same, but it would be something.

They needed to know that he loved them beyond measure—including the women that were now a part of their family. And Kane would leave Riley a note, as well. His cousin wasn't just family, she had become his best friend.

The stories the two shared had healed them both of pains neither realized they had. Riley was a beautiful soul who wanted nothing more than the love and acceptance of her family. She had that now.

Kane's arm tightened around Elise. It would be easier to leave her a letter, as well, but he wouldn't do that to her. She didn't have to save him. But by doing it, she'd created a bond that was unexpected and mind-boggling. It was stunning and wonderful, and an experience Kane wasn't sure he deserved.

He knew the odds of him coming out alive after his attack

on Delphine were slim. But if he took the priestess out so she couldn't hurt anyone else, then it would be worth it. Because he knew Delphine would go after Elise.

That alone propelled Kane to make his decision. He didn't want to leave Elise. He wanted nothing more than to remain with her forever, basking in her smile and the unconditional love she gave to others.

It was a good thing the asshole who hurt her had been caught. Otherwise, Kane would hunt him down and rip out his throat.

"I love you, too," he whispered before placing a kiss on her forehead.

Chapter 10

Elise came awake with a smile, nestled in Kane's arms. She'd lost count of how many times he woke her during the night to make love.

She sighed contentedly. Her body was lethargic after being loved so thoroughly. She wanted nothing more than to spend the day in bed with Kane. Unfortunately, she had clients coming in to see her.

"Hungry?" he asked as he kissed her temple.

She smiled up at him. "Starving."

"I'll start breakfast. How do waffles sound?"

"Amazing." She watched as he rose from the bed and walked naked to his clothes.

Damn, the man was a sight to behold. He easily put all the men sporting muscles and underwear on billboards to shame. Her gaze landed on his shapely ass as he tugged on his jeans. He didn't bother to button them or put on a shirt before he winked at her and walked from the room.

She stretched before she threw off the covers and got up. As she made her way to the bathroom, she caught sight of her reflection in the mirror. Pausing, Elise smiled at the woman staring back at her.

A woman who didn't care about the scars anymore. They were proof that she'd survived. Perhaps she should wear them like a badge instead of hiding them.

She hurried to her closet, shoving aside clothes as she searched for a short-sleeve shirt. She finally found one that was hidden in the very back. Elise smiled as she took it off the hanger and brought it and the rest of her clothes into the bathroom.

Her shower was quick in her haste to put on a piece of clothing she hadn't worn in three years. When she finally stared at herself in the mirror, she let her gaze rake over the scars on her arms that would now be visible to anyone. Yet, she wasn't afraid.

Being with Kane had done that for her. He had helped her to get past the fear that held her back. She didn't even want to think about her life without him. While they hadn't talked about the future, she was ready to try whatever it took, so long as they could be together. It was too early to tell him of her love, but she would hold it safely within her heart until the time came to share it.

She shook out her curls and walked from the bathroom just as Kane was finishing the waffles. Elise planted a kiss on his cheek and got out the syrup before pouring two cups of coffee.

To think, she had been happy living alone, just her and Mr. Darcy. She turned and saw the cat rubbing around Kane's legs, meowing up at him every so often. Mr. Darcy had fallen in love with Kane just as she had.

She sat at the table, ready to dig in to the breakfast. It wasn't until Kane sat across from her and she looked into his blue eyes that she knew something was wrong.

He ran a hand through his blond hair, shoving it back from his face before he reached for the syrup. She took a drink of coffee and watched him. He couldn't quite meet her gaze. The happiness she'd felt since waking was shattering right before her eyes.

"I like the shirt," he said, glancing up at her before putting a large bite into his mouth.

Elise set aside the cup and folded her hands on the table. Her appetite was now gone. "Whatever you have to say, just say it."

Kane slowly set down his fork and looked at her. "I was going to do it after our meal."

"I'd rather you do it now."

He gave a quick nod. "I'm going after Delphine."

She didn't need to ask if he were going alone. She knew he was. There was no point in arguing with him. Kane had made up his mind, and his stubbornness refused to allow him to consider another alternative.

"I'm surprised you didn't leave last night so you wouldn't

have to tell me."

His brow furrowed. "Is that what kind of man you think I am?"

"No." She took a deep breath and looked away. "I'm sorry. That was uncalled for. I just don't want you to go."

"I don't want to."

"Then don't," she said, jerking her gaze back to him. "Please."

He held out his hand, palm up. Elise put her hand in his, chills racing over her skin when his fingers curled around hers.

"If I don't do this, Delphine will remain out there, gathering strength. She may let us have a few years. Just enough where I'll think she's gone for good or moved on. Then she'll strike. She'll take you from me first. It'll be quick and vicious. And bloody. Someone else close to me will be next. She'll do it to remind me that she has the power to make me suffer. And to let me know that I walk this path alone. After that, she may or may not kill me. She likes to toy with people, and she's had plenty of opportunities to kill me and hasn't. It would be just like the mental bitch to keep me alive and remind me every chance she got about everything she took from me."

Elise's heart hurt for Kane. She might have tried to dismiss his words if she hadn't listened to his exchange with Mr. Perkins. It seemed Delphine's reputation exceeded well past New Orleans.

"Do you think you can win?" she asked.

Kane shot her a lopsided grin. "I'm sure as shit going to try."

"And if you do?"

He shook his head. "That's a conversation for when this is finished."

In other words, *if* he came back. Elise smiled and nodded. "Then go do what you have to do."

"There are some letters on your desk. Will you see that they're mailed?"

She glanced at her desk, frowning. "Did you sleep at all last night? I never even knew you got out of bed."

"I wrote them in bed with you."

That made her feel a little better. "I'll mail them."

"Your waffle is getting cold," he said and released her hand as he went back to eating.

It was all she could do to get half of the waffle down. Every bite stuck in her throat, threatening to come back up. Somehow, she ate and held a conversation with Kane as he told her the precautions to take.

All too soon, she was standing at the door with Kane, fighting back tears and the need to beg him to stay. She kept her back straight and her chin up, even though she was dying inside.

"If I lose, she'll come straight for you. If I'm not back in a day, head into the city to a bar called Gator Bait. One of my future sisters-in-law is a witch. She can help protect you," he told her.

She nodded.

He cupped her face and gave her a kiss that made her toes curl and her sex throb with the desire to feel him deep inside her. He sighed as he ended the kiss and looked down at her. "Be safe. Don't leave the house unless you have to."

"Come back to me."

His gaze filled with emotion as he pressed his forehead to hers. His lips parted as if he were going to say something, but he changed his mind at the last minute and gave her a hard, quick kiss before he was out the door.

Elise watched him as the tears fell unheeded down her cheeks. Mr. Darcy let out a plaintive meow and jumped on the windowsill to stare after him.

She wiped at her cheeks and turned away once Kane had disappeared into the trees. Elise walked to her desk and saw four letters—to Solomon, Myles, Court, and Riley.

Kane's last words returned to her, and she hurried to open her laptop to look up Gator Bait. In no time, she had the bar's website pulled up and her phone in hand, but she hesitated to call. Would they even believe her? Not to mention that Kane would be pissed if they showed up.

But she didn't care as long as he survived. That's what mattered.

Elise punched in the number. Her heart thudded in her chest as the line connected and it rang. Someone finally answered on the sixth ring.

The male voice on the other end gave her pause. "Can I

speak to one of the owners, please?"

"If this is a complaint, I'll be happy to listen."

She briefly closed her eyes and tried again. "I need to talk to one of the LaRues. This is about Kane."

There was a brief pause before the man said, "Hang on."

She was put on hold, music playing in the background. Elise stood and walked to the window to look at the last place she'd seen Kane. He had been so adamant about keeping his family out of his plan.

Listening to him describe the things Delphine had done to him and his family had been appalling. The woman was seriously deranged, and she needed to be stopped. It wasn't that Elise didn't believe Kane could do it, she just didn't want him battling the priestess alone. Elise wanted him back beside her.

Because she was protecting him.

Just as Kane was protecting his family.

Elise hung up the phone. As much as she believed Kane shouldn't face Delphine alone, she now understood why he had chosen such a role. He loved his family so much that he was willing to die for them if it meant that they could live free of such evil.

How could she stand in the way of that? She was thankful that she had been put on hold for so long. Otherwise, she would've told them everything. Elise cleaned up the kitchen and opened the doors to the clinic just as her first appointment arrived.

* * ★ ★ ★ * *

"She said it was about Kane," Court stated.

Solomon stood with his arms crossed over his chest as he looked from the phone to Myles and Court. "Did you ask her anything?"

"I put her on hold so all of us could hear what she had to say," Court said.

Myles leaned back in the chair and tossed another pencil into the ceiling above him. "We all knew Kane was alive, and now we have proof. I just want to know why he hasn't come home."

But Solomon knew. "Delphine. He's probably been tracking her."

Court shook his blond head. "He can't be so stupid as to go up against her alone."

"That's exactly what Kane plans," Myles replied softly.

Court gave a loud grunt. "Look at the times we've faced her. We managed to win each time, and some by the skin of our teeth, but every fucking time has been with the help of our allies."

"We know that," Solomon said. "And Kane knows that."

Court leaned his hands on Myles's desk. "Does he have a death wish? Is that what's got this bug up his ass?"

"He's doing it because Delphine came after Addison, Skye, and Minka. He's doing it for us," Myles said.

Solomon dropped his arms, a great weight settling on his shoulders. "I'm not losing him. I can't."

"*We* can't," Court corrected.

Myles nodded and leaned his forearms on his desk. "I don't know why this woman called, but we need to find her."

"Before it's too late for us to help Kane." Solomon turned as the back door to the bar opened, and their women walked in.

Minka's brown gaze collided with him, and she immediately hurried into the office. "What is it? What happened?"

"Kane," Solomon said. "A woman called about him, but she hung up before we could talk to her."

Minka grinned. "And you want me to find her."

"Her number, her address, anything," Myles said.

"I'm on it," Minka said.

Solomon watched her as Skye moved to Court's side, and Addison went to Myles. The LaRue family had just been the brothers for years, but now, it included their woman, friends, allies, and extended family.

Their cousins—especially Riley—had been waiting for another shot at Delphine. Maybe one last battle was in order to wipe the priestess out for good.

Chapter 11

Leaving Elise was the hardest thing Kane had ever been forced to do. With every step, he wanted to turn back to her, to run into her arms and hold onto her forever.

But how could he live with himself if he did? What right did he have to happiness while his family, friends, and innocents—and even him and Elise—would suffer from Delphine's continued rise to power.

So he would sacrifice whatever future happiness he might have had with Elise so others could live free of the priestess's wrath.

Kane didn't shift. Being in wolf form would give him an advantage with his heightened senses, but he had a plan. Even with Delphine's weres following at a distance, he chose not to shift.

Anger simmered through him. The weres weren't attacking him, because Delphine wanted him for herself. The show at Elise's house had been to get him outside. Well, he was there now, and Delphine would pay for everything she'd done to the LaRues, the Chiassons, and everyone else that had been hurt or killed by the priestess.

And the list was long.

Kane had grown up on the streets of New Orleans, but over the last couple of years, he had ventured far from the city into the bayous. While his cousins might know the bayous as well as they did, Kane was comfortable maneuvering the waterways, as well as avoiding the many dangerous animals that thrived in such a place.

He returned to the place he'd last seen the black mass. His gaze raked over the area where moss dangled from the limbs of the cypress trees. A fallen log was the resting place of a turtle on one side and an adolescent gator on the other.

The cloudless sky promised still air, and the temperatures, already in the upper nineties, guaranteed a sweltering afternoon. Just another typical day in Louisiana.

Kane's eyes moved slowly over the water. He counted four alligators floating beneath the surface, just their eyes visible. He saw another two on the bank. And all of them watched him.

The only way to the isle was through the water—a swamp infested with gators. There was no way he'd make it. And Delphine knew it.

A large, twelve-foot gator off to Kane's left hissed loudly. It was to warn Kane not to venture any closer. Gators were very territorial.

While Kane had no wish to tangle with the animals, he had to get to Delphine. Except she'd made sure to go to the one place he couldn't reach. She obviously wanted him out here, though, which meant she had some sort of plan.

"I'm waiting," he called toward the isle.

The sound of a woman's laughter—Delphine's cackle—floated on the air, causing icy fingers of foreboding to run down his spin.

Elise had just finished typing the notes about her last client when the door opened. "Be right with you," she said.

After she'd saved the notes, she turned to find the small room she used as her clinic filled with three tall men and three women. The men with their various shades of blond hair and the same blue eyes as Kane held her attention.

She didn't need to ask to know that these were his brothers.

"How did you find me?" she asked.

One of the men nodded instead of answering. "So, you know who we are?"

She lifted a shoulder in a shrug. "You have the same eyes as Kane."

"Where is he?" another of the men demanded.

The third sighed loudly and gave a shake of his head. "Please accept our apologies, Elise. We should've introduced ourselves first. I'm Myles, and the beauty beside me is

Addison."

Elise nodded woodenly at the realization that these people didn't just know who she was, they had found her. All because she'd placed a call to Gator Bait.

Well, Kane did say one of the women is a witch.

She halted her thoughts and paid attention as Myles introduced Court and Skye with her long, dark hair pulled into a ponytail, and then Solomon and Minka, whose curls lay over her shoulders.

"Hello," Elise said, unsure what to say next. "Kane isn't here."

Solomon's eyes looked to the door that led into her living room. "Why did you call?"

"Because I thought you should know what he's doing."

"Which is what?" Minka asked.

Elise leaned back against the counter and braced her hands on it as she looked into six different faces. This was Kane's family, the people who cared about him most.

Court's forehead frowned. "Elise?"

"Y'all better get comfortable," she said and motioned to the door. "I'll close the clinic so we won't be bothered."

While she flipped the *CLOSED* sign on the door, the others made their way into her house and took their seats. She rubbed her hands along her thighs as she stood before them, the denim scraping her palms.

She noticed each of them glance at her arms, but no one said anything about her scars. For her first day wearing a short-sleeved shirt, she was getting a dose of how others reacted.

Mr. Darcy walked to each of the brothers and sniffed them before coming to sit at her feet. Oddly, that small gesture gave her courage.

Elise swallowed and licked her lips. "I found Kane about five days ago. He was being attacked by a pack of wolves right out there," she said, motioning with her hand to the back yard and the bayou beyond. "I took my gun and fired it to run the others off. I saw the extent of his injuries and knew he would need help."

"Wait," Solomon said. "Wolves?" He and his brothers exchanged worried looks before he asked, "Am I to understand that you faced down wolves alone? With a gun?"

She nodded. "Foolish, I know, but I'm not one to let an animal suffer."

"So Kane was in his other form?" Court asked.

Elise grinned as she glanced at the floor. "I thought he was a large dog at first. He was unconscious as I dragged him to the door of my clinic to treat him. That's when he shifted."

"And you still tended him?" Addison asked.

Elise tucked hair behind her ear. "I love animals, but I'm not callous. And even though I didn't know what was going on, I had the means to stop the bleeding. Otherwise, Kane would've died."

"Thank you," Solomon said.

She looked out the window. "It was hours before he woke.

I convinced him to remain until his wounds were healed."

"You didn't know him," Skye said.

Elise glanced at her. "True, but I had glimpsed him in wolf form for weeks. He never harmed me. In fact, he stayed far away. And there was something in his eyes that told me I could trust him. While he was here, he told me who he was and explained what all of you do in the city."

"Kane doesn't share such things," Myles said.

She shrugged, wrinkling her nose. "Perhaps it was because I saw him shift."

"What made him leave?" Minka asked.

Elise bent and picked up the cat, holding the Siamese as he began to purr while she scratched his chin. "I left to get him some clothes. There were werewolves here when I returned. One nearly attacked me, but he stopped it in time. He said Delphine was the cause."

"I knew it," Solomon said and ran a hand down his face.

She rubbed her cheek against Mr. Darcy's head. "Kane put up wards around the house. Then, this morning, he told me he had to go after Delphine. I tried, unsuccessfully, to talk him into contacting all of you. He said each of you had someone, and since he was the cause of all of this, he would fix it."

"I'm going to kill him," Court said angrily, his worry over his brother filling his blue eyes.

Myles covered Addison's hand and squeezed it before he looked at Elise. "Obviously, you called to tell us what he was doing. Why did you hang up?"

Elise's gaze returned to the window as she remembered Kane walking into the bayou. "I wanted to help him, but my reasons were selfish. I want him back."

"Because you love him," Minka said.

Elise nodded. "While I was on hold, I thought about all the things Kane had told me about each of you and the battles you've fought with Delphine. This is his way of ensuring that none of you have to fight her again and can live happily together."

"Not without him," Solomon said.

Skye's head cocked to the side. "And he has you."

Elise gave Mr. Darcy one more rub before setting him down. "He's doing this for me, as well. He said the first thing Delphine would do was come after me."

"He's right," Court murmured.

Solomon got to his feet and moved to stand at one of the windows looking out. "I'd do the same thing if I were in Kane's shoes. But while I understand his thinking, I won't allow him to fight her on his own."

"Then we find him now," Myles said as he stood.

Court snorted loudly and rose. "As if you even need to ask my opinion."

"Wait," Elise said. "You should know that the weres who attacked Kane and me aren't from the Moonstone Pack. Kane believes they're Delphine's followers. People she turned."

Court rolled his eyes. "Damn, this bitch just doesn't know

when to stop."

Minka jumped to her feet and hurried to Solomon, who turned to face her. "I'm coming with you."

"That might be wise," Elise said. "Kane mentioned that Delphine was now a black mass instead of a person."

Addison's brow puckered into a frown as she looked at the others. "Does that mean she's more powerful?"

Minka shrugged. "It's a possibility."

"It could be a trap," Skye said.

Elise nodded. "Kane thought the same thing, but he said it had to be done."

"It does," Myles stated.

Court raised his brows as he glanced at his brothers. "Without a doubt."

"So, now what?" Addison asked. "Surely, the three of you aren't going to go barging out there."

"Four," Minka interjected as she looked at Solomon.

Elise watched as the eldest LaRue and his witch stared at each other for a long time. Solomon blew out a breath, his silent agreement obviously done in protest.

Minka grinned before she faced Addison, Skye, and Elise. "Kane did a pretty good job warding the house. I'm going to add more, but the three of you should remain inside."

"I think you should, as well," Solomon said.

Minka shot him a look but didn't reply. Elise wrung her hands as the witch walked onto the porch and stood at the door with her hand on the wood for a moment before she moved out of sight.

"Minka's very good," Addison said.

Skye nodded. "You'll be safe long after we're gone."

As if Elise needed a reminder that Kane would no longer be in her life. She was about to reply when she caught Addison staring at her arms.

Elise moved them behind her and shifted so that it would be difficult for anyone to see them. She was used to people being in her clinic, but not her house. Her small house felt even tinier with the others inside. She wanted to rush out and look for Kane herself.

The time they'd had together was amazing and all too fleeting. She hadn't comprehended just how special those few days could be, but she was coming to realize it now. And she ached to have more.

"It's going to be all right."

Elise blinked to find Minka before her and the others out on the porch. The witch's brown eyes held a wealth of kindness as she smiled. "I know you don't know us, but trust us, please."

"I'll help however I can to find Kane," Elise said.

"I've no doubt."

Elise remained in the house as the six spoke, the lovers saying their good-byes before Solomon, Minka, Myles, and Court followed the same path Kane had taken hours earlier.

Chapter 12

"Oh, Kane. I knew it would be you that came for me."

It felt as if Delphine's voice were all around him. The blue skies were blocked out, the entire area darkening as if a blanket had been pulled over it.

Kane fisted his hands as the urge to shift slammed into him. He knew that, somehow, Delphine was responsible.

"I could've killed you at any time these past months," she said. "I've been waiting for you to come to me."

He looked around, noting that the bayou had gone eerily silent. "Show yourself."

"Hm. I don't think so. I quite like this."

"What do you want, Delphine?"

It felt as if something caressed his face. "You."

He jerked back, revolted at the thought of her touching him. "I'm not in the mood for jokes."

"I'm not joking," came her terse reply.

Kane drew in a deep breath and attempted to figure out the priestess's angle.

More laughter floated around him. "I've got you wondering now."

"You kill."

"Yes, and I'm good at it," came the whisper close to his ear.

Kane hated the fact that she was seemingly all around him, and he could do nothing about it. Proving that she was right—she could kill him anytime.

"George put you in this form," he said.

She made a sound somewhere between a hiss and a growl. "Don't ever mention his name again. It took everything I had to hold back his magic, but it was you who dealt the final blow. We work well together."

"If he had gotten the upper hand on you, it would've been your neck I bit," Kane replied.

She chuckled. "It's true, he did something to me. I couldn't take solid form. That hindered me for a while. I couldn't control anything, not even my magic."

Kane could've kicked himself. If only he had found her then, it would've been so easy to kill her.

"But then I learned just how powerful I am in this form. I'm no longer limited as I was with a body. I move faster, and can make myself as big or small as I need."

Fucking wonderful. The lunatic was now a certified psychopath. That's just what everyone needed. And if she were difficult to find, he imagined she'd be even harder to kill.

"You don't look happy," she said with a laugh.

"I came to kill you. My job is a little harder, but I'm up to the challenge."

Once again, something slid along his cheek—and then down his chest to his cock. "Well, you can certainly try. Tell me, Kane, do you know why I cursed you to go after Ava?"

The fact that Delphine was bringing up Ava, who was now engaged to his cousin, Lincoln, was disturbing. Even more upsetting was that Delphine wanted to discuss the very thing that had altered his life.

"Because I pissed you off," he stated and moved away from her.

"I let you believe that was the reason. In truth, I'd been watching you and your brothers for some time. I saw the potential in you."

He was repelled by the notion that she'd watched any of them that closely. "Potential for what?"

"Blood. Mayhem. Death...evil."

Kane wanted to gag, to hit her with all the rage that was currently built up in him.

Suddenly, her voice came from behind him, her mouth close to his ear once more. "Look what I turned you into. You're a killing machine, Kane. You're focused, determined. I gave that to you."

He whirled around to get away from her, even though he knew he couldn't. She was the one blocking out the sun, which meant she might very well be able to keep him right there forever. Had he fallen right into her trap?

"No!" he bellowed. "I nearly killed my cousins and the woman Linc fell in love with! I'm like this for one purpose only—to kill you!"

She laughed long and loud. "Believe what you want. Your actions speak louder than your pitiful words."

Kane had never felt such hate before. "And Riley? What was she?"

"Someone I needed. Or, at least, I believed I needed her. Turns out, I got what I wanted without her."

Was Delphine implying that she could take over New Orleans now? God, Kane hoped that wasn't the case. His brothers—hell, the entire *city*—weren't prepared for that.

No doubt everyone had gotten used to Delphine being absent from the city, putting everyone in a false state of peace. The fallout from her return would be epic. The all-out war between the factions would spill from New Orleans into neighboring towns.

And the death toll would gain national attention.

This had to be contained. Now. Any way possible. Which meant it was all up to Kane.

"Do my words upset you?"

He fought to control his anger. "You know they do."

"I know how much you love your family. They mean a lot to you, don't they?"

"They mean everything."

He heard the smile in her words as Delphine said, "That's

exactly what I'm counting on."

He was fucked two ways from Sunday. There was no doubt about it now. And no matter how hard he looked, he couldn't find a way out of the situation.

Had Elise been right? Should he have brought his brothers along? Or was he justified in doing this alone so only he had to suffer whatever was coming?

As soon as he thought of Elise, that was the only thing on his mind. But he quickly shoved her aside. He had no idea how much Delphine's powers had grown, and he didn't wish to test anything yet.

"You speak as if you have a proposal," he said.

There was movement in the dimness, as if everything became a little darker. "You've proven your worth by working with me to kill George. It showed me that there is no one better to stand by my side as I rule New Orleans than you."

"No," he answered.

"You might want to hold up before you reply. You've not heard my full offer."

"I'll not work with you."

Something wound around his body. He looked down but could see nothing. "Oh, you will," she said.

He didn't like her confidence. There was only one thing that could make him do whatever she wanted—threatening those he cared about.

And the bitch knew it.

"Oh, I see you've figured it out," she said, a smirk in her

voice. "I knew you were smart."

"Spell it out for me anyway," he demanded.

"Fine, but I don't like your tone. You best curb that attitude. Quickly."

She was about to get more than sarcasm. She would get the monster she thought she created.

"Join me, stand beside me as I take over New Orleans. The LaRues have kept everyone in line for years. Instead of your family, I'll take over. With you by my side, there will be no uprisings, no war, because they'll see that I have the approval of your family."

She was certified, bat-shit crazy. There was no denying it.

The darkness around him shifted into the form of Delphine. Kane blinked against the harsh light of the sun suddenly visible again. He stared into the priestess's black eyes. Her black hair hung to her waist in rows of small braids. She wore a white gauze dress that showed the outline of her body and was a stark contrast to her dark skin.

She smiled and held out her arms. "A little show of what my power can do. Why not join me? If you swear to serve me, I give you my word that no one—including me—will ever harm your family again. Not your brothers, their women, or their children. Not your cousins or their families. I'll even throw in the veterinarian who patched you up. They'll live happily and be safe. All you have to do is join me."

There was a catch in there somewhere, Kane just couldn't see it yet. Asking her would be pointless, though. Delphine was willing to give him a lot to have him stand with her.

Her brow quirked, agitation making her lips thin. "You hesitate?"

"I'm wondering why you want me? If you need some lackey to stand at your side, you have dozens of followers. Hell, you even cursed some to be werewolves."

She cut her eyes to him. "They chose that option. And I want you, not just anyone."

"Right," he said with a nod. "Because I have the ability within me to do evil."

"Yes."

He laughed. "Everyone does. Just as everyone," he paused and wrinkled his nose at her, "well, almost everyone, can do good. There's another reason you want me. I won't give you an answer until you tell me what that is."

"I can kill everyone you ever cared about in an instant," she threatened.

"You've been doing that for years, so that doesn't pose the threat it might have, had you told me after murdering my parents."

Her black eyes narrowed on him. "You will be my enforcer."

"Of course," he said with a snort.

"That displeases you?"

He crossed his arms over his chest. "Your weres nearly killed me the other day."

"And they've been punished for it. They were only supposed to wound you, but their hatred was too great."

"You mean you lost control of them."

The way her nostrils flared told him he'd hit a nerve. Good. He wanted to hammer the shit out of it.

She tilted her head, her braids falling to the side. "They didn't do much damage to you the second time, did they?"

"They would have killed the vet."

Delphine smiled suddenly. "Nice try, making me believe you don't care about her by not saying her name. I'm not buying it for a second. I saw how quickly you came to her aid."

"What did you expect?"

She tsked loudly. "I thought you were smarter than that. By staying with the beautiful Elise, you gave me enough incentive to kill her. If you valued her life, you would've walked away from her immediately. Apparently, evil actually rules you."

Kane didn't want to believe that, but he knew that staying with Elise put her at risk—yet he had remained. What kind of fool was he? Had he done it on purpose like Delphine suggested? Had he known Elise could die because of it?

Delphine closed the distance between them. "You belong with me, Kane. I can show you power the likes of which you can't begin to fathom. No one will ever question you again. On top of that, your family will be safe. What more could you want?"

Elise. He wanted Elise, but it didn't matter because he knew that no matter what, he'd never have her. Delphine would see to that.

"The answer is on your face," Delphine said as she put her hand on his chest. "All you have to do is say the words."

He stared into her black eyes and thought of all the times he had tried to kill her, of all the times she had taken the life of one of his friends or allies.

"Say it," she urged, her smile growing tight.

His family had made a vow to protect New Orleans from evil. He would be going back on that if he agreed to Delphine's terms. But his brothers would have a life free of battle and death.

"Join me!" she shouted.

"Don't do it, Kane."

He whirled around and saw his brothers standing shoulder-to-shoulder, ready to fight. So much for him fighting Delphine alone.

Chapter 13

ELISE LOWERED HER CELL PHONE TO THE DESK. SHE marked her calendar after finishing the last of the calls to reschedule the rest of the day's appointments. Thankfully, they'd all just been check-ups—not to say that an emergency wouldn't show up.

She had been woken in the early-morning hours many nights to tend to injured animals. But that was just part of her job.

She looked over at Skye and Addison. Skye was flipping through a magazine, while Addison absently petted Mr. Darcy, who was curled up in her lap, as she stared at the floor.

"I feel so useless," Elise said.

The women looked at her. Addison smiled sadly. "It's something I struggle with constantly."

"It's easier for Minka," Skye said. "Being a witch allows her to get right into the mix of things."

The chair creaked as Elise leaned back. "I've never been in

a situation like this. I'd like to think I would stand and fight, but to be honest, I'd probably run."

"We all want to run," Addison admitted.

Skye nodded, her lips twisted ruefully. "Delphine is terrifying. We've both faced her, and it's only because of the LaRues that we're still alive."

Addison jerked her chin to the degrees framed on her wall, as well as some of the pictures of the places she had worked. "You have impressive skills by the looks of it. Why remain out here? You could make a killing in New Orleans."

Elise placed her hand over a scar on her arm. She'd made the decision not to hide them, but she wasn't sure if she was ready to tell everyone her story. But this new her had to start with tiny steps. And this was a good one.

"I was attacked one night as I left New Orleans. Someone ran me off the road. My attacker wanted to rape me, and I fought back. It got me these when I protected my face," she said as she held up her arms. "The people here saved me. It was an old Creole woman who healed my wounds, and I never left. I've found a place in this community."

Skye grinned as she set aside the magazine. "I believe you're meant to be here. We can't thank you enough for helping Kane."

"I just want him to win against Delphine."

Addison sighed. "We all do. I pray every night for a future without her in it."

"I can't even imagine such a day, not after everything we've been through with her."

Elise listened to the two and understood fully why Kane had gone after the Voodoo priestess himself. She hated the thought of him facing her alone, but Kane was doing it out of love for his family. She only hoped he outwitted Delphine.

"I've got a bad feeling about all of this," Skye said as she rose and paced the living room.

Elise frowned because she'd had that same feeling since Kane left. "How so?"

"Delphine has a certain modus operandi," Addison said. "She doesn't wait around to kill those she wants out of the way."

Elise's hands were shaking as she placed them on her desk and rose to her feet. "There was ample time for Delphine to attack. Days, in fact."

"That's what I've been going over in my head," Skye said. "You told us how the weres attacked Kane. If she had wanted him dead, they would've killed Kane and you without a second's hesitation."

"But they didn't." Elise swallowed, her chest feeling tight. "Nor did they do anything on the second attack."

Addison's face was lined with concern. "She could have. I know that she's powerful enough to kill someone with just her mind."

"So why spare Kane and me?" Elise asked.

Skye crossed her arms over her chest. "That's a very good question. There can only be one reason."

"She wants him for something." The idea made Elise sick to her stomach.

Addison dropped her head back on the sofa. "Not again. After everything we went through to get Riley back."

"Delphine won't take Kane's memories," Skye said.

Elise frowned when Skye's dark gaze turned to her. "What?"

"She'll use you against him," Addison said. "She'll use all of us."

"And here I thought she'd left us alone because Kane warded the house." Elise pulled in a shaky breath. "Tell me there's more to do than sitting around waiting."

Skye snorted and looked away, which was answer enough.

Suddenly, Mr. Darcy jumped off Addison's lap to the arm of the sofa. He let out a hiss while staring out the window to the back yard and then growled low in his throat.

"I do believe we'd better prepare," Elise said.

Addison quickly stood. "Minka put spells on the house. No one can get in unless we let them inside."

"She's right," Skye told Elise. "We'll be fine."

Elise wished she could believe that. She'd feel better if Kane were with her, but she imagined he had his own problems to deal with.

"Come back to me, Kane," she whispered as the first werewolf stepped out of the trees.

"Holy fuck," Court mumbled.

Solomon silently agreed as they watched Delphine's form shift into something resembling black smoke before it wrapped around Kane, blocking him from their view.

"We've got to do something," Myles said.

Solomon was trying to think of the best way to attack when Delphine—and Kane—disappeared.

Court raked a hand through his hair in frustration. "What just happened? I mean, did y'all see that?"

"Of course, we did," Myles snapped.

With his brothers looking to him for answers, Solomon did his best to hide his growing fear and unease. "She wasn't surprised to see us."

"It was like she wanted us here," Myles said.

Court put his hands on his hips and shook his head. "If Delphine can change into that black smoke thing now, then we are screwed."

Minka walked out of the copse of trees behind them. "She's more powerful now."

Damn. That's not what Solomon wanted to hear. "Kane didn't fight her."

"She didn't give him a choice," Court said.

Myles blew out a breath. "Perhaps. But he wasn't happy to see us."

"Don't condemn Kane yet," Minka warned.

Solomon glanced at her before facing his brothers. "She's

right. We don't know what Delphine told Kane. When we got here, they were talking."

"Yeah. Talking. Because that's what Delphine does." Court dropped his arms to his sides and turned away, cussing beneath his breath.

Solomon's gaze met Myles's. "What do you think?"

Myles slowly shook his head. "I know Kane well enough to know that he'll do whatever it takes to keep us out of another battle with Delphine. Even if that means sacrificing himself."

"I know." And that's what made Solomon so heartsick.

He should've seen this coming. He should've tried to talk to Kane about it instead of putting it all on Riley.

"We need to call Riley," he told them. "I want to know everything she and Kane talked about while they were living together."

Court immediately headed back toward Elise's house. Halfway there, they all came to a halt. Solomon grabbed Minka and pushed her behind him.

"What is it?" she whispered.

He turned his head to her. "Weres."

Court kicked off his boots as he pulled his shirt over his head. Minka turned away as Court removed his jeans and shifted before running off ahead of them toward the right. Myles gave Solomon a nod before he undressed and shifted and then disappeared to the left.

"Do it," Minka told him.

Solomon hesitated, but he knew just how powerful his

witch was. He gave her a quick kiss and hastily removed his clothes before he called forth his wolf.

Once in were form, he looked up at Minka, who stood beside him, her hand sinking into the fur at his neck. Her gaze was directed straight ahead, in the direction of Elise's house. He didn't need to ask to know that magic was already building within his woman.

She took a step forward. He remained beside Minka, and with every step, words began to tumble from her lips as the spell she cast grew.

"Shit," Skye said when she saw the werewolf.

Almost immediately, two more joined the first. Elise went for her shotgun, but by the time she got it loaded, loud growls reached her.

"The boys are here," Skye shouted.

Elise hurried to the window and watched as two wolves attacked the three werewolves facing the house. She had no idea which one was which as they came at the others from opposite sides. The clash was fierce and brutal.

Both Skye and Addison were shouting and clapping. Elise stood with the shotgun in her hands, wondering what she should do. What were Court and Myles doing back at the house? Had they located Kane?

"Oh, hell," Addison murmured.

Elise's gaze jerked to the sight of Minka walking from the tree line with a huge white wolf by her side who was obviously Solomon. Minka's lips were moving, her gaze locked on the three interlopers.

Solomon crouched down, his lips peeled back to reveal his long fangs as he growled and jumped into the fray along with his brothers.

Minka remained, her arms now lifted out to her sides and her face turned to the sky. Elise looked up at the clouds to find them darkening and slowly swirling into a cone shape.

Suddenly, more werewolves surrounded them. Elise ran to the front of the house and saw them coming at them from all sides. She rushed back to Skye and Addison, her heart hammering in her chest.

"Minka needs to get inside. She's going to die out there," she said.

Skye shook her head of black hair. "The weres won't be able to get close to her. Watch."

Elise's gaze was drawn to the witch. Just as Skye predicated, every time a werewolf tried to attack Minka, they were struck down by lightning.

"Her powers continue to grow," Addison said, a smile in her voice.

Elise wasn't sure how to feel about any of it. She didn't fully understand what was going on, and it didn't help that this was her first time in such a battle—and meeting Kane's family. She was doing her best to keep her composure, but she couldn't stop thinking about Kane.

"*Elise!*"

Her head jerked to the side. That was Kane's voice. Hadn't the others heard it? She looked to Skye and Addison, but both were focused on their men.

"*Elise. I need you. Please.*"

"Did y'all hear that?" she asked, her eyes locked on the door to her clinic.

Skye clapped. "That's my man! Go, Court! Kick some ass, baby!"

Elise glanced at the women before she walked to the door and opened it. She peered inside, but there was no sign of Kane. Her hands were clammy as they gripped the gun.

"*Elise, Delphine has me trapped. I need help, but my brothers can't hear me.*"

"Kane? Where are you?" she asked as his voice grew fainter. "Kane!"

She looked over her shoulder again. There was no telling how long the battle in her backyard would last. But there was one thing she knew—Kane needed help.

"Skye! Addison!" she called, but neither heard her over their yells to their men.

She looked at the door leading outside. What was she going to do? She had no magic, no ability to shift. Perhaps she could use that to her advantage. Maybe she could surprise Delphine and get off a shot at the priestess's head.

Or she could be walking to her death.

Chapter 14

"WHY ARE YOU FIGHTING THE INEVITABLE?"

Kane briefly closed his eyes. He kept asking himself that same question. Delphine continued to push her proposal, and at first glance, it seemed perfect.

Too perfect.

Well, aside from the fact that he'd give her his support. It would almost be worth it if his family were free of such a person, but if she were in control of the city, would they really be safe?

Or would Delphine find some way to kill them?

Kane shoved aside the moss that hung from a low limb as he looked across the water to where his brothers had been. He'd tried to call out for them, but whatever Delphine did to block out the sun had also prevented his voice from reaching them. By the time the black mass left him, he found himself on the isle, and his brothers gone.

"I don't like to be kept waiting," Delphine snapped.

He turned his head to her and glared. "And I don't like being forcibly taken."

"We weren't finished with our conversation."

"What did you do to my brothers?" he demanded.

She rolled her eyes. "Really? We're in discussions, and you think I harmed them?"

"It sounds exactly like something you'd do."

Delphine grinned. "It does, doesn't it?" She shrugged, sighing loudly. "However, I promise that I did nothing to them. I kept you hidden until they were gone."

"Then where are they?"

Her lips curved into an evil smile. "I may have sent my wolves to keep watch on the house."

"If anything happens to my family or Elise, I'll never help you."

"I've done this long enough to know how far I can push things, Kane. My weres are merely there as a reminder of my power. They won't harm anyone, though they will protect themselves if assaulted."

He snorted and crossed his arms over his chest as he faced her. "No doubt your weres put themselves in just such a threatening position so they would be attacked."

"They have orders to do nothing but watch the house."

"Right. And I'm the Pope."

Delphine laughed as she eyed him. "Why not agree to my terms? I've given you everything you could want."

"Except my freedom. I'll be shackled to you."

A black brow rose. "Careful. My patience is running thin."

"It's the truth."

"What's wrong with siding with the most powerful being in New Orleans? Nothing. No one will dare go against you. I'll allow you to keep the silly rules your family instigated."

Kane laughed and dropped his arms. "You can't be serious? Those 'silly rules' as you call them, will stop you, as well."

"They'll apply to everyone but me and my followers."

"So my so-called power will be in name only." Figured.

She blew out a harsh breath. "Look at the big picture. New Orleans is just the first step. I've much larger plans. I'll take over the state, and eventually, the country."

"The country?" he repeated, shock reverberating through him.

Delphine gave him a knowing look. "You don't think I can do it?"

"I believe there are others out there who would fight you to keep you from doing exactly that."

"And they'll die. I've already got the djinn on my side. The vampires are waiting for you to side with me as I've promised them you would."

Kane was shocked to his very core. While he and his family had been trying to keep themselves alive and stop whatever scheme Delphine had going on, she'd been moving pieces behind their backs, altering the game altogether.

The mistake they had made was thinking she was only after the LaRues and Chiassons. It had never been just about them, and if they had stepped back and looked around, they might have seen it.

All these months, they'd thought they were winning against Delphine, when in fact, while they could claim the skirmishes, she would win the war.

"Why did you take Riley?" he demanded. "Was she just a diversion?"

Delphine shook her head. "Riley was meant for so much more. She was stronger than I realized. I should've kept a tighter rein on her."

"It was George who ruined it for you."

She cut her eyes to the side, anger in every feature. "He was obsessed with her. If he'd just waited, he could've had her and anyone else he wanted."

To hear Delphine talk so blithely about Riley made Kane's blood boil. Yet he kept it hidden. There was no way Delphine would get away with everything she had done.

The only thing stopping him from attacking her now was that she'd kill him without Kane being able to get any information to his brothers.

But the thought of siding with her, even as a sham, might be the end of him.

There were no other choices for him. If he refused her, Delphine would kill him then go after his family and Elise. They wouldn't survive. His cousins would be next. All the while, Delphine would continue her quest to rule the city, state, and country.

Who would be left to stop her? Who would dare rise up against her?

The only reason the witches had helped them in the past was because they worked as a team. Hell, even the Moonstone Pack was scarce. It was only the LaRues who held that tenuous pact together.

If the LaRues were killed, the witches would go into hiding. The Moonstone Pack would scatter like before. Even if he didn't side with Delphine, the vampires would eventually fall to her. It was simply a matter of time.

Then the way would be clear for Delphine to gain all she wanted.

"I need an answer," the priestess demanded.

Kane turned his head to the side and watched a crane snag a fish from the water before flapping its white wings and flying away.

"Let me talk to my brothers."

"No," she replied.

He swiveled his head toward her. "If I don't tell them why I'm taking your offer, they'll attack you, and you'll kill them."

"I can stop them in other ways. Wiping their memories would be easy enough," she said flippantly.

Kane gawked at her. "Don't you dare."

She gave him a flat look. "If you're going to leave your family, wouldn't it be easier for them if they didn't remember you or anything they've been doing all these years? Let them believe the paranormal is something for movies and books."

"Will you do the same for me?"

"If you'd like."

Kane turned his back to her and braced a hand on a tree. No matter which way he looked at it, he couldn't find a way to best Delphine. Not now, at least. And if he didn't do it right away, and she gained more power, the harder it would become—until it eventually became impossible.

"Your answer, Kane," she demanded.

He was stuck between a rock and a hard place. No matter what, his life would be Hell. At least he could give his brothers and cousins some peace to live a normal life and raise their families.

"I want to talk to my brothers."

"Give me your answer first."

Shit. He was going to hate his life.

"Kane."

He frowned. What was Delphine's hurry all of a sudden? She had been patient, coaxing even, but all that'd changed over the last few minutes.

Just as he was turning to ask Delphine, his gaze spied movement across the bayou. His heart fell to his feet when he saw Elise.

"What is the meaning of this?" he asked as he whirled to face Delphine.

Agitation lined her face. "I'd hoped you would agree without needing that final push. Seems I was wrong."

★ ★ ★ ★ ★ ★ ★

"I can do this. I can do this," Elise told herself as she marched through the bayou to the place Kane's voice had led her.

She saw him across the water, standing with his hand on a tree. A woman with long, black hair and dark skin marking her exotic beauty was behind him.

Delphine. So that's what the Voodoo priestess looked like.

Elise wanted to take aim with her gun, but Kane was too close to her, and at this distance, she might very well hit him instead of Delphine.

She walked closer, watching as Kane turned to Delphine, and they began arguing. Was that a good sign? Damn, she didn't know. Elise knew very little about what to expect. Maybe she shouldn't have followed the voice.

But she had been so sure it was Kane. Now, not so much.

"Elise, leave!" Kane bellowed.

His words halted her. It confirmed her worries. Kane hadn't led her here. Delphine had. That made Elise despise the woman more than ever—and she didn't even know the priestess.

Her blood ran like ice when she heard the low grumble of a growl behind her. Elise slowly looked over her shoulder to find a werewolf.

Kane walked to the edge of the small mound of earth in the middle of the water but drew to a stop when an alligator rose up from the water before him.

There was no going back for her. And she was fine with that. From the moment she'd saved Kane in his wolf form until now, she was where she belonged—with him.

Elise raised her shotgun to her shoulder. She took aim at Delphine, but before she could squeeze off a shot, the gun was knocked out of her grasp, and she found herself tossed unceremoniously to the ground.

When she looked up, she gazed into Delphine's black eyes. Even Elise could feel the power that flowed through the priestess. No wonder so many feared her.

Delphine grasped her jaw with fingers that bit into Elise's cheeks. "You stupid fool. I can't believe you fell for my trick. Since when has Kane ever projected his voice like that?"

Elise tried to tug Delphine's hand away, but she couldn't budge her even an inch. "You knew I would come for Kane."

"Because you love him," Delphine stated with disdain.

Elise grinned through the pain. "And I knew you'd come over here for me. Who's the fool now?"

Chapter 15

"ELISE!" KANE BELLOWED WHEN DELPHINE TACKLED HER to the ground.

He had to get to Elise, to save her from certain death. Kane stepped into the water, only to jump back before a gator lunged for his foot.

"Fuck," he grumbled, his gaze jerking back up to Elise.

Kane quickly scanned the area, looking for a place to cross that didn't have alligators waiting to take a bite out of him. He moved from one side of the tiny isle to the other, but it was as difficult to get off, as it was to get on.

No wonder Delphine had chosen it.

Frustration and fear pounded through him, slamming his heart against his ribs. He'd been about to agree to Delphine's proposal, to take her at her word that she would make sure his family and Elise were safe and unharmed.

How stupid was he to believe anything that came out of Delphine's mouth? She manipulated and lied her way to whatever she wanted. If anything, Kane should've known he couldn't trust her.

"Elise!" he shouted again.

He'd be shattered if she were killed—and nothing would ever put him back together. How could he bring her into this unwinnable war? How could he have dared to think about his own pleasure for even an instant?

A howl he knew well sounded to his left. Kane's head snapped in that direction as a silvery white wolf came into view with Minka by his side.

"Solomon," he whispered.

Minka walked to the edge of the bayou and held her hands out. Kane stared in amazement at the ripples moving over the water as alligators swam away.

Kane didn't waste any time hurrying into the water. The edge dropped off quickly, and he swam to the opposite side where Minka and Solomon awaited him. Just as he was about to run to Elise, Minka grabbed his arm.

"Wait," she cautioned.

He glared at her. "Are you insane? Delphine is going to kill her."

Solomon growled in response.

Minka rubbed Solomon's head and told Kane, "Your Elise has a plan, and it's a good one."

"What?" he asked, unsure if he'd heard her correctly.

Minka gave him a quick smile. "Trust us. And be ready."

He gawked at Minka, who hurried out of sight. Kane's

head swung back to Delphine and Elise before he looked at Solomon. Kane had no idea where Court or Myles were, but if his brothers liked the plan, then it had to be good.

Solomon trotted off, and Kane grudgingly followed. He glanced back at Elise one last time, praying she knew what she was doing.

"Nice try," Delphine said with a smile.

Elise continued to attempt to pull the priestess's hands away from her jaw, to no avail. Delphine was frighteningly strong. Elise didn't know if it was magic or not, but it didn't matter. She just needed to get free.

"No one can mess with another's mind like I can," Delphine stated. "But I will give you props for the attempt."

Elise laughed, though the sound came out more like a bleating cow. "Attempt? I've done more than that."

Delphine's black eyes narrowed as she squeezed harder. Then she looked up. Even with dots beginning to edge Elise's vision from lack of oxygen, she still enjoyed seeing Delphine's smile vanish when she caught sight of Minka.

Elise dragged in a gulp of air as Delphine's grip suddenly disappeared. She could hear Minka and the priestess talking, but she couldn't make out their words. Elise was losing consciousness. She fought to remain awake, but it was becoming more difficult.

"Stay with me."

Elise rolled onto her side, frowning at the sound of Miss Babette's voice in her head.

"That's it, my girl. Stay with me," Babette said.

Elise felt as if she were floating between worlds. She opened her eyes, but she was no longer lying on the ground. She was in Babette's house, gazing down at her blood-soaked body as the old woman spoke calmly while she and another frantically tried to stop the bleeding.

She didn't understand what was going on. Elise recalled very little of the night she was attacked. It wasn't until days later when she woke up in Babette's house that they told her what had happened.

So, what was she seeing now?

Elise blinked, and the scene changed. Her many injuries had been stitched, and Babette sat on the side of the bed as she put salve on the wounds before wrapping them in bandages.

"You still have much to do, my girl," the woman said. "You're needed, though he won't realize how much until everything may be lost."

Elise shook her head. What the hell was going on? But even as the thought went through her mind, she concentrated on Babette.

The old woman sat back and sighed loudly. "I've seen what's to come, Elise. You have great strength in you, though you haven't recognized it yet. He will show you it's there. But you're going to have to use it. You can't hear my words now, but when you need them the most, they will come to you."

Elise reached out to see if she could touch Babette, and in the next instant, found herself once more on the ground. She dug her fingers into the grass as the words reverberated in her head.

Without a doubt, she knew Babette had been speaking of Kane, and while the old woman hadn't said Delphine's name, this was the event she must have seen.

Elise rose up on her hands and knees and ignored her bruised jaw as she swallowed. Minka and Delphine were going head-to-head with their magic, and while Minka was holding her own, she was weakening.

After getting to her feet, Elise looked for Kane on the isle, but he wasn't there. She smiled. Another part of the plan had worked.

Elise had the feeling someone was watching her. She turned her head to the side and saw Babette standing about fifty yards away. All around her lay dead werewolves who would no longer be coming to Delphine's aid.

Kane wanted to dive into the battle. He and his brothers waited, hidden, for the signal. Not that he knew what the signal was. As soon as he followed Solomon, he'd shifted and joined his siblings. But he didn't need words to know that this was their final stand.

They would either kill Delphine or die trying.

Kane snapped his jaws. The longer he waited for a piece of the priestess, the more annoyed he became.

Solomon issued a low growl of warning that someone approached from behind them. As one, the four of them turned and crouched down, ready to attack.

Kane was shocked to find Griffin, Alpha of the Moonstone Pack. Behind him were others of the pack. The last time they had seen Griffin, he'd been helping Delphine. Granted, the priestess had his sister, but still.

Griffin raised his hands. "We're here to watch and act as backup if necessary. We've taken out several of Delphine's weres. I know you might not believe me, Kane, but we've got your backs."

Solomon gave a nod and turned back to the fight. Myles and Court did the same. But Kane bared his teeth to Griffin. He'd been the one to befriend Griffin and convince him to return to New Orleans. Kane went out of his way to bring the Moonstone Pack back together, and he and his family had been betrayed.

It was something he didn't easily forgive—or forget.

An Alpha didn't show submission easily, but Griffin bowed his head to Kane. "I'm sorry. I've spent these last months earning my pack's trust again. I'll do whatever it takes to earn yours. I lost my sister, Kane. She was the only reason I helped Delphine. I can't change the past, but I can prove myself. My pack has surrounded the area. Delphine won't get past us."

They didn't know that the priestess could shift into nothing more than a bit of smoke, and Kane didn't have time to tell them now. He turned to Delphine and Minka when he heard a shriek of anger.

Kane's gaze sought out Elise. He was happy to see she was on her feet again. Her gaze was off to the side, and by her smile, she saw something or someone she recognized.

Solomon began to pace when it was evident that Minka was weakening against the onslaught of Delphine's magic. Something had to be done, and quickly.

Kane started forward, but Myles jumped in his way.

Delphine was going to win. Again. Elise couldn't imagine a world where the priestess ruled all. Because Elise realized that this was the final battle, the conclusion of years of skirmishes between the LaRues and Delphine.

Elise took a step toward Minka when the witch dropped to her knees and struggled to keep her magic going. Elise looked around for Kane and his brothers. This was when they should join in. Why weren't they?

She spotted the reason a moment later when Babette walked to stand beside Minka. The old Creole woman lifted her chin and glared at Delphine.

"I warned you never to return here," Babette said.

Delphine laughed as she dropped her hands, halting the

magic she had directed at Minka. "Babette. I thought you'd be dead by now."

"You tried hard enough, but I don't die easily."

Elise looked back and forth between them, paying special attention to the tension between the two women.

Delphine raked her gaze over Babette. "You look...old, sister."

Elise's mouth dropped open. You could've knocked her down with a feather she was so surprised.

Babette slowly shook her head. "Reverting to barbs, just like when you were a kid because you didn't have the intelligence to argue."

"No, I had the kind of power that really mattered," Delphine retorted.

Babette smiled sadly. "You took the wrong path. I hope you enjoyed the power you had because you're about to lose it."

"Oh, I don't think so. No one can touch me now."

Babette raised a brow, a grin forming as Kane, Solomon, Myles, and Court moved in a semi-circle behind Delphine. "You were always looking ahead, Delphine, grasping for things that were out of reach, which made you miss what was right in front of you."

Elise frowned. She knew those words. She wasn't sure how, but she knew them, had lived them before...somehow. Her gaze slid to Kane to find him watching her. In his yellow eyes, she saw recognition of Babette's words, as well.

She turned her head to Babette and then Delphine. As she did, a vision of sorts formed. Elise saw Kane lunge at Delphine and sink his teeth into her throat.

"I'm done with this!" Delphine bellowed. "All of you will die this day."

A chill ran down Elise's spine as Babette cut her eyes to her. Elise knew Delphine had to be kept in her current form, but how? Minka was so weak, she could barely lift her head, and Babette didn't seem to have any magic at all.

Babette gave a small, barely discernable nod, as if to tell Elise to continue her train of thought. Then time slid to a crawl as Babette turned her head to Delphine and held out her arms. In the next instant, Babette was encased in flames.

"No!" Elise screamed as Babette flailed about before collapsing.

Minka was able to use her magic to put out the flames, but it was already too late. Babette was dead.

Rage burned through Elise. She looked around for her shotgun as yelps of pain mixed with growls of warning came from the LaRues. Her head jerked to the werewolves to find that Delphine had Myles, Solomon, and Court pinned down with her magic as she glared at Kane.

Elise briefly met Kane's gaze. She forgot her shotgun and rushed Delphine, but the Voodoo priestess spun around to face her before Elise could do anything.

"I'm going to make Kane watch as I kill his family, but I'm saving you for last," Delphine announced.

The priestess's body began to grow hazy, and Elise realized she was shifting into the black mass again. The image of Kane killing Delphine with his jaws around her throat replayed again.

"No," Elise stated. "You'll remain here. In your human form."

Delphine's laugh cut off in the middle as she became solid once again. Her gaze held a wealth of anger and retribution as she looked at Elise. "What did you do? You've no magic?"

Elise smiled coldly. "That's right. I don't have magic, but what I have is command over you."

Delphine took a step back. "That's not...possible."

"Babette once told me that I have control over what's on my land. It's why you never fought the LaRues at any place they owned. It was always someplace one of your followers retained or was owned by the city. But you made a mistake here," Elise said as she moved a step closer. "This is my land."

Fear reflected in Delphine's black eyes as the truth settled over her.

Elise grinned as she saw Kane crouch down and get ready to attack. "You were right. You are done. And I know just the wolf to finish you."

Delphine turned, her scream cut off as Kane's powerful jaws locked around her throat. There was a snap as he broke her neck before dropping her lifeless body.

Elise's legs gave out, and she crumpled to the ground. She couldn't believe it was over. Kane walked to her and shifted.

She winced when she heard his bones popping back into place.

His yellow wolf eyes faded to bright blue, and then she was in his arms. She closed her eyes and savored the feeling of being held by him.

"I thought I'd lost you," he said as he leaned back to look at her. "How did you do that?"

Elise looked to Babette's charred body as Court, Myles, Solomon, and Minka walked to them. "When Babette tended me after my attack, she told me about this day. Not in exact words, but enough. I didn't remember any of it until today when she appeared."

"She was Delphine's sister," Minka said. "I didn't think Delphine had family."

Kane shook his head. "Babette saved us."

Myles and Court suddenly took off running toward her house for Addison and Skye. Minka shot her and Kane a smile before walking away with Solomon. Elise took a deep breath as Kane linked his fingers with hers.

"You kicked ass," he said with a sexy grin.

"I didn't do anything other than what Babette showed me needed to happen."

Kane shrugged a shoulder. "I beg to differ. That took serious courage. You were magnificent."

She smiled, happiness flooding her. "Magnificent, huh?"

"Hell yeah. Is it any wonder I love you?"

Her heart stopped as she blinked at his confession.

He skimmed his knuckles down her cheek. "I think I've loved you since I woke up in your house. You...inspire me. I want to spend every day for the rest of my life showing you how much I love you."

She swallowed and rose up on her knees to cup her hands on either side of his face. "How do you always know just what to say?"

"With you, it's easy."

She grinned and pressed her lips to his for a soft kiss. "I love you."

His smile was blinding as he got to his feet and lifted her into his arms as he spun them around.

The evil that had ruled his life for so long was gone. Something else would take its place eventually because it was the way of the world. But for now, there was peace and happiness.

And love.

Epilogue

Two weeks later...

Complete. That's how Kane felt now. He lifted the longneck beer to his mouth for a swig as he watched the women of his family surround Elise. She smiled at him, and he felt as if his heart would burst.

Solomon came up beside him. "You got a good one."

"I know," Kane said with a grin.

"I suppose we'll be seeing much more of her?"

Kane looked at his brother and nodded. "I believe so. Especially since I'm moving in with her."

"Hot damn," Court said as he came up, slapping a hand on Kane's shoulder. "I knew it."

Kane frowned as Myles walked up, followed by their cousins Vincent, Lincoln, Beau, Christian, and Marshall, Riley's fiancé. "What are you talking about?"

"We made a bet," Beau said.

Christian nodded.

"When you and Elise were going to move in together and where," Lincoln said with a grin before he took a drink of his beer.

Vincent elbowed Linc as he shook his head. "Ignore them, Kane."

"Bullshit," Marshall said with a laugh. "You were the first to place a bet, Vin."

They all laughed. When the laughter died down, they each looked around, realizing how precious their time was together, and how easily Delphine could've won and destroyed it all.

"Laughing without me is a crime," Riley said as she walked up and put her arm around Marshall. "I am engaged to a sheriff, you know. So don't piss me off, or I'll have you arrested."

Beau rolled his eyes. "Oh, God. That again?"

"Ah, yeah," Riley replied sarcastically.

Marshall winked at Riley before pulling her close for a kiss.

The circle expanded as Olivia went to Vin, Ava to Linc, Davena to Beau, Ivy to Christian, Addison to Myles, Skye to Court, and Minka to Solomon.

Kane held out his hand for Elise as he pulled her against him. This was their family now. Regardless of what was to come, they would stand together.

He held up his beer and looked around. "A toast to

family. For as long as I can remember, it was just me, Court, Solomon, and Myles. Fate brought us back to our cousins, and both families have been blessed that each of us has found love. May these bonds that hold us together only strengthen with the years."

"Hear, hear," the others said in unison.

Everyone began talking at once, but Kane didn't hear them. He pulled Elise close for a kiss, his heart nearly bursting with happiness. His love for her grew every day. It seemed impossible that he could love her more, but he did.

"Okay, okay," Riley said loudly to gain everyone's attention. "I know we're just getting this party started, but we did close down Gator Bait for the night so we could all be together."

Ivy chuckled as Davena and Skye exchanged looks.

"Sweetheart, you're making everyone nervous," Marshall said.

Riley rolled her blue eyes. "No, I'm making the guys nervous. Well, too bad, because now that we're all here, we're going to schedule all the weddings." Kane laughed as the women pulled out calendars they must have hidden in their shirts. Elise was so shocked, she spilled some of her beer on herself.

"I don't know why you're laughing," Christian said to Kane. "Take notes, dude. Your time is coming, and Riley is a damn drill sergeant when it comes to this."

Kane felt Elise's gaze on him. He looked at her and wrapped an arm around her shoulders before rubbing his thumb along her cheek. He raised a brow in question.

She shrugged, grinning all the while.

"Too soon?" he whispered.

Elise glanced at the others flipping through their calendars. "It doesn't hurt to take notes."

"You mean, let them make the mistakes, and we have the perfect wedding?"

She laughed, nodding. "I like the sound of that."

He stared into her green eyes and turned to face her. "You make every day wonderful. I can't wait to see what the rest of our lives looks like."

"Ohhh," she said as she rose up on her tiptoes and pressed her lips to his. "You always know what to say."

He turned and dipped her for a steamy kiss as his family shouted encouragement behind him.

No matter what monsters or evil came at them, they would fight it as a family. And there was no greater bond than that. Together, the Chiassons and LaRues were unstoppable.

And it was time the supernatural world realized that.

Thank you for reading *Moon Bound*. I hope you enjoyed it! I love getting to step back into this paranormal world.

If you liked this book – or any of my other releases – please consider rating the book at the online retailer of your choice. Your ratings and reviews help other readers find new favorites, and of course there is no better or more appreciated support for an author than word of mouth recommendations from happy readers. Thanks again for your interest in my books!

Donna Grant
www.DonnaGrant.com
www.MotherofDragonsBooks.com

LOOK FOR THE NEXT BOOK IN MY DARK KING SERIES – HEAT COMING JANUARY 30, 2018!

Clearview, Texas
Three weeks before Christmas

THIS SHIT COULDN'T BE HAPPENING. ABBY HARPER'S heart thumped against her ribs as she turned into the parking lot of the sheriff's department. She parked and opened her car door, only to have her keys drop from her shaking hands. It took her three tries to pick them up because she couldn't get her fingers to listen to what her brain was telling them.

Along with the fact that her brother had been arrested, her mind couldn't stop thinking about the money she was losing for leaving her job early to find out what happened. Which meant that there was a real possibility that she would have to choose between paying for electricity or groceries next week.

She hunkered into her coat, bracing against a blast of cold air as she hurried to the door of the building. As soon as she was inside, the heat engulfed her.

Coming through the speakers overhead was the old Willie Nelson and Waylon Jennings song *Momma, Don't Let Your Babies Grow Up to be Cowboys.*

The irony wasn't lost on her. The problem was, she'd done everything she could. But Clearview was in cattle country. That meant there were cowboys everywhere—as well as rodeos that happened too frequently to even count.

Abby licked her lips and walked up to the counter and the glass window. A man in a uniform slid back the pane and raised his blond brows in question. His look told her he didn't care what had brought her there or what sad story she might have.

"Hi," she said, her voice squeaking. Abby cleared her throat and tried again. "Hi. I'm here about Brice Harper."

"You don't look old enough to be his mother," the man stated as he reached for a file.

After all these years, Abby should've been used to such a response. But she didn't think a person ever got used to such things.

She forced a half smile. "I'm his sister, but also his legal guardian."

"And your parents?"

If it had been anyone but a sheriff's deputy, Abby would've told them it was none of their business.

"Dad died years ago, and our mother ran off. But not before she gave me legal guardianship of my brothers."

The man's dark eyes widened. "You have another brother?"

"Yes."

As if she needed another reminder that she was failing at raising her siblings.

"Through that door," the deputy said as he pointed to his left.

A loud beep sounded, and Abby dashed to open the door. She walked through it to find another police officer waiting for her. Despite Brice's reckless nature and the rowdy crowd he hung with, this was her first time at a police station.

And, quite frankly, she prayed it was her last.

Nothing could prepare anyone for what awaited them once they entered. The plain white walls, thick doors, locks, and cameras everywhere made her feel as if the building were closing in on her. And that didn't even take into account all the deputies watching her as she walked past.

She wasn't sure if being taken back to see Brice was a good thing or not. Wasn't there supposed to be something about bail? Not that she could pay it.

Her thoughts came to a halt when the deputy stopped by a door and opened it as he stepped aside. Abby glanced inside the room before she looked at him. He jerked his chin toward the door.

She hesitantly stepped to the entrance. Her gaze landed on a familiar figure, and relief swamped her. "Danny."

"Hi, Abby," he said as he rose from his seat at the table in the middle of the room.

His kind, hazel eyes crinkled at the corners with his smile. He walked to her then and guided her to the table. All her apprehension vanished. Not even the fact that he also wore a sheriff's deputy uniform bothered her. Because she'd known Danny Oldman since they were in grade school.

He'd run with the popular crowd at school because he'd been one of the stars of the football team, but Danny never forgot that he'd grown up in the wrong part of town—next door to her.

"I'm so glad you're here," she said.

His smile slipped a little. "What Brice did is serious, Abby."

She pulled out the chair, the metal scraping on the floor like a screech, and sat. "No one has told me anything. Brice refused to speak of it. He just told me to come."

"Perhaps you should be more firm with him."

The deep voice sent a shiver through her. She hadn't realized anyone else was in the room. Abby looked over her shoulder to see a tall, lean man push away from the corner and walk toward her.

His black Stetson was pulled low over his face, but she got a glimpse of a clean-shaven jaw, square chin, and wide, thin lips. It wasn't until he stopped across the table from her and flattened his hands on the surface that she remembered to breathe.

"Abby," Danny said. "This is Clayton East. Clayton, Abby

Harper."

It was a good thing she was already sitting because Abby was sure her legs wouldn't have held her. Everyone knew the Easts. Their ranch was the largest in the county. The family was known to be generous and welcoming, but that wasn't the vibe she got from Clayton at the moment.

Then it hit her. Whatever Brice had done involved the East Ranch. Of all the people for her brother to piss off, it had to be them. There was no way she could compete with their wealth or influence. In other words, her family was screwed ten ways from Sunday.

Clayton lifted his head, pushing his hat back with a finger. She glimpsed strands of blond hair beneath the hat. Her gaze clashed with pale green eyes that impaled her with a steely look. No matter what she did, she couldn't look away. She'd never seen so much bottled anger or anguish in someone's stare before.

It stunned her. And she suspected it had nothing to do with her brother or the ranch but something else entirely. She wondered what it could be.

"No," she said.

What should've been internal dialogue came out. Clayton's blond brows snapped together in confusion. She glanced at Danny, hoping that her outburst would be ignored. It wasn't as if Clayton needed to know that her history with men was . . . well, it was best left forgotten.

When she looked back at Clayton, she was arrested by

his rugged his rugged features. He wasn't just handsome. He was gorgeous. Skin tanned a deep brown from the sun only highlighted his eyes more. His angular features shouldn't be appealing, but they were oh, so attractive.

She decided to look away from his face to gather herself but realized that was a mistake when her gaze dropped to the denim shirt that hugged his wide, thick shoulders. The sleeves were rolled up to his forearms, showcasing the edge of a tattoo that she almost asked to see.

Abby leaned back in her chair, which allowed her to get a better glimpse of Clayton East's lower half. Tan-colored denim hung low on his trim hips and encased his long legs.

He was every inch the cowboy, and yet the vibe he gave off said he wasn't entirely comfortable in such attire. Which couldn't be right. He'd been raised on the ranch. If anyone could wear such clothes with authority, it was Clayton East.

Danny cleared his throat loudly. Her gaze darted to him, and she saw his pointed look. Wanting to kick herself, Abby drew in a deep breath. Just as she was about to start talking, Clayton spoke.

"Cattle rustling is a serious offense."

Abby's purse dropped from her hand to the floor. She couldn't have heard right. "Cattle rustling?"

"We picked up Brice trying to load cattle with the East brand on them into a trailer," Danny said. "Those with him ran off."

She was going to be sick. Abby glanced around for a

garbage can. This couldn't be happening. Brice was a little reckless, but weren't most sixteen-year-olds?

Though she knew that for the lie it was. She'd known from the moment their mother walked out on them that it would be a miracle if Brice graduated high school. He acted out, which was his way of dealing with things.

"I . . . I . . . ," She shook her head.

What did one say in response to such a statement? Sorry? I don't know what's wrong with him?

Danny propped himself on the edge of the table and looked down at her, his hazel eyes filled with concern. "You should've come to me if Brice was out of control."

"He hasn't been, though," she argued. And that wasn't a lie. "Brice's grades have improved, and he's really straightened up."

Danny blew out a long breath. "Is there anyone new he's been hanging around with?"

"No," she assured him. "Not that I've seen."

After the last incident when Brice was about to enter a house that his friends had broken into, he'd sworn he wouldn't get into any more trouble. Abby truly believed that the brush with the law had set him straight.

Her heart sank as she realized that her brother could very well go to jail. She knew she was a poor substitute for their mother, but she'd done the best she could.

"What happens now?" she asked, racking her brain to come up with memories of past shows she'd seen to indicate what would happen next. "Is there a bail hearing or something?"

"That depends on Clayton."

Just what she needed.

But Abby was willing to do anything for her brothers. She sat up straight and looked Clayton in the eye. "My brother is young and stupid. I'm not making excuses for him, but he's had a hard time since our mother left. I'm doing everything I can to—"

"You're raising him?"

She halted at his interruption before nodding. "Both Brice and Caleb."

He stared at her for a long, silent minute.

Abby wasn't too proud to beg. And she'd even get on her knees if that was what it took. "Please don't press charges. I'll pay back whatever it is you've lost with the theft."

"Abby," Danny said in a harsh whisper.

"Is that so?" Clayton asked as he crossed his arms over his chest. "You're really going to repay my family?"

Abby looked between Clayton and Danny before returning her gaze to Clayton and nodding. Her throat clogged because she knew the amount would be enormous, but if it meant her brother wouldn't go to jail, she'd gladly pay it.

"There were a hundred cows stolen. Thirty of them were recovered when your brother was arrested, which leaves seventy unaccounted for. Let's round it to $2000 each. That's $140,000. Not to mention that each of them is about to calf. Each calf will go for a minimum of $500 each. That's an additional $35,000."

Oh, God. She would be paying for the rest of her life. And she was fairly certain Clayton wanted the payment now. How in the world was she ever going to come up with that kind of money?

But Clayton East wasn't finished. He had yet to deliver the killing blow.

"Then there's Cochise, one of our prized bulls. He's worth $100,000."

She put a hand over her mouth as her stomach rebelled. She really was going to be sick, and at the moment, the idea of vomiting on Clayton East sounded tempting.

There was no way she could come up with $275, much less $275,000. Worse, Clayton knew it. It was written all over his face.

Danny rose to his feet and stood at the end of the table. "Abby, you need to get Brice to tell you where the rest of the cattle are."

The words barely penetrated her mind. She stared at the metal table, her mind blank. Usually, she was able to think up some way to get her brothers out of whatever mess they'd gotten into—and there had been some real doozies.

She'd toiled through various jobs until she landed a position at the CPA company where she was currently employed. Despite the fact that she worked sixty hours a week, they wouldn't put her on salary because that would mean they'd have to give her health insurance.

Even with those hours and every cent she scraped together, it still didn't cover their monthly bills. But the one thing she'd promised her brothers was that she would take care of them.

And she had.

Up until today.

She scooped up her purse and stood before facing Danny. "I'd like to see my brother now."

It took everything within her to walk out of the room without giving the high and mighty Clayton East a piece of her mind.

NEVER MISS A NEW BOOK FROM DONNA GRANT!

Sign up for Donna's newsletter @ tinyurl.com/DonnaGrantNews

Be the first to get notified of new releases and be eligible for special subscribers-only exclusive content and giveaways. Sign up today!

ABOUT THE AUTHOR

New York Times and *USA Today* bestselling author Donna Grant has been praised for her "totally addictive" and "unique and sensual" stories. She's written more than seventy novels spanning multiple genres of romance including the bestselling Dark King stories. Her acclaimed series, Dark Warriors, feature a thrilling combination of Druids, primeval gods, and immortal Highlanders who are dark, dangerous, and irresistible. She lives with two children, a dog, and three cats in Texas.

CONNECT WITH DONNA ONLINE:
www.DonnaGrant.com
Facebook: facebook.com/AuthorDonnaGrant
Twitter: @donna_grant
Instagram: instagram.com/dgauthor
Pinterest: pinterest.com/donnagrant1
Goodreads: goodreads.com/author/show/1141209.
Donna_Grant

Printed in Great Britain
by Amazon